Tales with a Twist

Ethics, Dilemmas and Points of View

Discussion, Writing, Improvisation

by
Greta Barclay Lipson, Ed.D.

illustrated by Susan Kropa

Cover by Susan Kropa

Copyright © Good Apple, 1991

ISBN No. 0-86653-609-4

Printing No. 987654321

Good Apple
1204 Buchanan St., Box 299
Carthage, IL 62321-0299

SIMON & SCHUSTER *A Paramount Communications Company*

Tales with a Twist

Dedication

There were three empty spaces in the family, waiting to be filled, when fate played its poetic, random game and brought us Susan, Lorene and Jane.

Three young women—different, yet alike: intelligent, fair featured and spirited! We claim their elegance among the more expansive gifts bestowed on us. In honor of that twist of fate, we gratefully dedicate this book to them.

We love them, not for comely grace alone.

GA1328

Table of Contents

My enduring gratitude to Geraldine N. Barclay for editing the original manuscript.

Introduction

These tales are explorations of mystery, danger, comedy, and human nonsense from sources old and new. The stories in this book were deliberately chosen because they are dramatic incidents with strange and evocative endings. Each vignette lends itself to a search for answers to difficult questions. Every selection is the basis for a lesson plan and activities which include discussion, improvisation, and writing.

Is a thief less a thief for stealing food? Is it true that what you don't know won't hurt you? Is there truly a sucker born every minute? Is your anatomy your destiny? Do we reap as we have sown? No single answer can resolve a dilemma or a conflict but therein lies the learning!

It would be foolish to deny the role of fate in the scenario of our lives or to deny the inexorable forces of nature or the unremitting effect of social class on all of us. There is so much that is in place for each of us at the time of birth that, some argue, we are almost programmed for our destiny. Others believe that we are the controllers of our destiny. Included in this calculation, of course, is the effect of the country in which we live—and our relative freedom, repression, education, or personal drive.

The eternal conflict between fate and free will has been examined throughout human history and is found, most notably, in the great plays of the ancient Greeks. In modern times the uncertainty of fate is characterized in works such as Robert Frost's poem, "The Road Not Taken." This selection is a cogent piece because it suggests that we do have some choices, and we do make daily decisions which influence our lives. To the degree that we can shape our own fate, we must learn to ask questions, assess information, make decisions, and set standards for ethical behavior.

In my secondary school, of olden times, I believed that my English teachers really taught us about life as reflected in books. It seemed that literature teachers dealt with realistic concerns, about which we were invited to express an opinion and were taken seriously. Literature was a medium of socialization which helped us understand something of what the world was all about, because—more than history or science or mathematics or "the facts" as we know them—literature captures the essence of human behavior.

Educators are conduits of the human experience with all that implies—and significant stories are the magical materials with which they forge an awareness of the real world outside of the classroom. The stories are the stuff of life, exceeding the limits of what any one of us could possibly encounter personally (or would want to).

When literature does its job, it shows all of us how people and events work in society. One hopes that a sharpened perspective and new insights will help us understand much more about ourselves and enable us to do much better in taking charge of our own lives.

How to Use This Book

Each of the twelve tales in this book is a dramatic incident which acts as a basic lesson plan for activities. The format is consistent and flexible:

- The Story

- Point of View—Discussion Questions

- Improvisation—Role-Play Variations

- Writing Suggestions

- Student Comment

When stories are evocative, they invite analysis and speculation through discussion. Among the many implicit questions in the selections are the following: What is the real issue in the story? What motivates people to do what they do? Why are the events disturbing or funny? Is anybody or anything accountable for the circumstances? If the decision were left to you, how would you have done something differently than the characters? And indeed—what were the alternatives? We learn slowly that all choices have consequences, and we can only speculate about what the outcomes may be. And perhaps, just perhaps, it is possible to stand up to fate.

Here, as always, the teacher is the guide from, "... the intelligent progression from cocksure ignorance to thoughtful probability."*

---

*Ashley Montague and Edward Darling. *The Ignorance of Certainty* (New York: Harper and Row, 1970).

Chapter 1
Lady in the Cave

GA1328

Chapter 1
Lady in the Cave*
Synopsis

Emmis is a very serious man who leaves his home and family to search for the meaning of truth. He travels over the far reaches of the land when, haggard and depleted, he finds the Lady in the Cave on a mountaintop. Her name is Verity—and she is eternally dedicated to truth. Aged and frail, her hair is wispy and her tired countenance shows the stark inroads made by the hardships of life. Emmis stays on as her student to learn the mysteries of truth. After a year of study and revelation, he prepares to leave and gratefully asks Verity what he can do to repay her kindness. Her response fills Emmis with consternation!

Retold by Greta B. Lipson, Ed.D, from *Favorite Folktales from Around the World*, edited by Jane Yolen (New York: Random House, 1986).

Chapter 1
Lady in the Cave

The Truth Shall Set You Free

Retold by Greta B. Lipson

There once was a man by the name of Emmis who was highly respected in his town. He was known to be a most honest and upstanding citizen who was trusted by all. He was, however, a very serious person and was always searching for the meaning of truth. A man such as Emmis was rarely heard to laugh, and he was not much fun to be with. As a matter of fact, he had become terribly boring in his zealous pursuit of the truth and was generally avoided by those who were more light of heart!

Emmis plodded along—never satisfied that the ultimate secrets of honesty had been revealed to him. The fact that others were not so consumed was of little interest to him. One day he went to his wife and said, "I really must satisfy my yearning to know about the meaning of truth and how it is acquired; I believe I must go in search of the answers before I become too old to travel—for I have no way of knowing how long my quest will take."

His wife Martha was a strong and patient woman. After listening carefully to what her husband expressed, she responded with understanding, "I know how you have felt about this for your entire life, and I know how important this matter is to you. Do what you have to do and we will love you all the same. We shall all look forward to your return no matter how long it takes you." Some say she must have been relieved to be rid of her husband with his constantly furrowed brow and persistent musing!

GA1328

Emmis left his home carrying a small knapsack since he did not want the burden of many belongings. He traveled very long distances each day and left his home further and further behind. He crossed rivers and streams, lakes and oceans, always looking for the truth. He visited small towns and villages and big bustling cities that were larger and more filled with people than anyplace he had ever imagined. He walked through the silence of dense woods and majestic forests in his fruitless search—but nothing was revealed to him. His threadbare clothes hung on his tired frame announcing to anyone who saw him that he was an exhausted man searching for something that was forever elusive.

One strange day Emmis found himself, unaccountably, at the very top of a mountain. He was drawn to a cave at a dizzying height, and when he looked into the cool, compelling darkness he saw the form of an old, bent woman. He knew intuitively that he had arrived at the place he had sought for so long. "Are you the Lady Truth?" he asked softly.

"Yes, I am," she answered slowly.

"May I come in and speak with you awhile?" he hesitated.

"Anyone who travels such a hard route to find me is always welcome," she responded. "Come in, please."

It was then, when Emmis was in the cave, that he saw by the firelight how very old and frail she was. Her skin was like wrinkled leather pulled over the fine bones of her face. She had few teeth in her mouth and her hair hung in pathetic, wispy strands. Her eyes were dimmed with age but she had a spiritual aura that softened her image with a magic luminosity.

GA1328

They spoke haltingly because the man was shy, until he was so overcome with her wisdom that he was moved to ask a favor of her. "There is so much to talk about, and you have so much to teach me—may I stay? Will you accept me as your student?"

"Of course," she responded, and he was soon at his ease in her presence when she said, "My name is Verity. Please call me by my name."

Emmis stayed with her in the cave, barely noticing the passage of time, because he had so much to learn. He was an eager student and each day he sat and listened and asked questions. Finally one remarkable year had passed. Satisfied that Verity had imparted to him all that he could absorb, he announced that it was time for him to take his leave.

5

GA1328

Standing at the mouth of the cave, Emmis was filled with emotion. "I am eternally grateful to you for all you have taught me about truth. Is there something I can do for you—some way I can repay you?"

Without hesitation Verity responded. "Since you are kind enough to offer," she said, "there is a favor I would ask of you."

She looked into his eyes. He waited. "When they ask about me—tell them that I am young and beautiful."

6

GA1328

Lady in the Cave

Point of View—Discussion Questions:

1. Why would Verity, who had devoted a lifetime to the examination of the meaning of truth, ask her student, Emmis, to tell an outrageous lie about her age and appearance when he returned to civilization?

Possible Answer:
Perhaps Verity was being honest with herself and realistic about the values of our society. We place a great premium upon outward physical beauty—and put much less emphasis upon the internal qualities of people which are not so quickly discernable. Neither age, nor intelligence, nor wisdom rank as important in the popular culture as youth and beauty—however we may protest to the contrary.

2. Explain how Emmis could tell everyone that Verity was beautiful and be absolutely honest about it.

3. When in search of meaningful or profound answers, why do many stories take the reader to distant and exotic places such as mountaintops, caves, and other remote areas? Is there more purity to be found away from the clamor of civilization?

4. Is truth constant, unwavering, and absolute, or does truth change in different contexts, eras, or circumstances? (In ancient times, the sun was thought to revolve around the earth. People were punished for contradicting that truth.)

GA1328

Lady in the Cave

Improvisation—Role-Play Variations:

1. Play the story as it reads. Include questions and answers in the dialogue which could have taken place in the cave. Partnerships or groups may participate in the role play after some planning sessions.

2. Entrepreneurs and assorted business types hear about Verity and set up a carnival atmosphere for profit at the top of the mountain where the Lady in the Cave resides. They advertise that the truth can be bought. Concerned citizens come to protest the commercialization of the message. They do not believe that the truth is an article of merchandise which can be purchased like groceries or other commodities. They believe that such offers are misleading and offensive to honest people.

3. The local politicians denounce Verity at a political rally because they are not sure what she is all about and what damage she can do to their reputations or their plans for the future. They are afraid of a crusade against corruption in government and what could be revealed in the name of truth and honesty in civic affairs. Public officials will appear at a speaker's forum to defend their turf. Each one intends to attack "the truth" as a public menace.

Lady in the Cave

Writing Suggestions:

1. Write two paragraphs. In the first paragraph explain some of the advantages of telling the truth all of the time. In the second explain the disadvantages. What could happen to a dedicated truth-teller in the course of a school day? Is there a time for a "little white lie"? What exactly does that mean? When is silence golden?

2. As part of a group effort, write an after-school special which deals with the theme of honesty in school, business, or public life. What are some of the significant problems with dishonesty in a school environment and how does it affect students as individuals?

3. Verity is described as frail and elderly as the Lady in the Cave. Are elderly people generally described in stereotypic ways? The term *ageist* describes a prejudicial attitude toward old people. Sharpen your sensitivity toward this view. Keep a TV log of commercials and other media advertising which uses older people. How are older citizens portrayed? Are they vigorous, bright, and productive citizens or are they infirm, foolish, and peculiar? What conclusions do you draw from your findings? Can one generalize about this group of people? Does wisdom and honesty come with age? Explain.

4. "To me, old age is always fifteen years older than I am." This is a quote from the American financier and adviser to Presidents, Bernard M. Baruch, on his eighty-fifth birthday, August 1955. In your view, how old is old?

 GA1328

Chapter 1
Lady in the Cave
The Truth Shall Set You Free
Student Comment

Characters: Verity, the Lady in the Cave
            Emmis, the truth seeker
            Martha, his wife

. . . .

In a paragraph express your feelings about any aspect of this story which you liked or disliked. How would you have changed it?

Alternative: Now that the story has been discussed, explain the proverb above from your point of view.

. . . .

_____

_____

_____

_____

GA1328

Chapter 2
You *Can* Take It with You

GA1328

Chapter 2
You *Can* Take It with You
Synopsis

Boris and his wife, Sophie, work very hard in the family delicatessen. They have three children. The oldest boy is Leon, the middle son is Daniel, and their little girl is Becky. As young as they are, the children work hard in the store and are, for the most part, uncomplaining. They do, however, have a conflict with Papa who doesn't understand the modern idea of giving children an allowance. Indeed there is an ongoing conflict over money. The family experiences its first tragedy when Papa becomes seriously ill. On his deathbed Boris asks his faithful wife, Sophie, to fulfill a strange and seemingly impossible promise.

GA1328

Chapter 2
You *Can* Take It with You

A Promise Is a Bond Sanctified by Trust

By Greta B. Lipson

Boris had worked desperately hard all of his life and was finally rewarded with a moderate sense of security. His little delicatessen prospered and Sophie and the children worked by his side after school and on weekends without a single complaint—except maybe once in a while when the children agitated for an allowance. It was clear to them that other children, who didn't work nearly as hard as they, got allowances, and it just wasn't fair!

The boys, Leon and Daniel, put up stock and waited on customers and even little sister Becky could make change and do odds and ends to keep things in order. When they approached their father, he would say, "Have I told you about the Great Depression, when grown men were selling apples on the street for a nickel apiece and people were digging into garbage cans to find something to eat?"

And the children would answer patiently, "Yes, Papa. We heard about the Great Depression."

"Did you know that we were so poor that all we could afford was to rent a bedroom with kitchen privileges from the Allegretti family?"

GA1328

Leon, the oldest, was the most realistic and the most resigned, "I told you guys to forget it," he advised his brother and sister. "Papa never heard about allowances in his whole entire life. So forget the allowance, 'cause he's never going to say *yes*. It means nothing for me, nothing for you, Daniel, and nothing for Becky."

"He's stingy," the two youngest muttered, "That's all there is to it. That's his biggest problem." They had it all figured out.

When their mother, Sophie, heard them, she always defended her husband staunchly. "Your father doesn't understand why children should get money for doing what they are supposed to do for the family. That's not the way he grew up! Maybe you don't understand the way he feels. Maybe you can't understand because you've always had it so good. Someday when you grow up you'll see what it's like to struggle to make a living."

"But, Ma," they whined.

"That's enough already. I don't want to hear anymore. When you get older you'll appreciate what he's done for you." She had heard enough.

"But Ma, I don't get it."

"You don't have to get it," she scolded. "Just respect your father."

GA1328

Very soon after, the children and Sophie were overwhelmed with sadder and more important matters. Their father fell gravely ill and the course of his sickness was quick and relentless.

The family hovered at his bedside. This was the first test of their strength, as the children, in a frightened huddle, listened to the hushed conversation between their parents. Sophie held her husband's waxen, cold hand. He whispered to his wife in a failing voice, "I have one final favor to ask of you."

"Anything you want," she replied softly.

"Will you promise first, Sophie, before I ask you?"

"I have never broken a promise to you, Boris, through all our years together." Sophie leaned toward his face with loving concern.

Boris's voice weakened. He seemed strangely disconnected from them but focused all his strength on this moment. As if from a remote place they heard him say, "I want you to promise that you will bury me with all my money."

There was a horrified silence. The children froze with the portent of Papa's last request. The security of their future would be dashed to pieces on the whim of this strange sick man who was their father. Suspended in time, they looked into their mother's impassive face and, disbelieving, they heard her say, "I promise you faithfully, my husband, to honor your last request. Now rest."

GA1328

Boris closed his eyes in serene contentment and left them for his eternal sleep. The children wept near hysteria—partly over the loss of their father and partly over the immensity of Sophie's promise to Papa. "Oh, Ma," they wailed, "how could you do this? Why did you agree to make such a promise? What will happen to us now?"

"It was your father's deathbed wish. There will be no further discussion." They knew her heart was breaking, but her face was stone.

"But you won't do it will you, Ma? You wouldn't bury him with his money." Sophie's silence was her only reply to her children.

The funeral was small and Malkivich's Funeral Home was adequate to the occasion. Neighborhood friends came and some old-time customers from the delicatessen. The eulogy was brief and respectful. It would have been a fitting service for any of the hardworking people in the community.

It was time for the ritual to end. The casket was to be closed after the family said their last good-byes. Leon was the tallest, and he could see his mother, strong and loyal to the last, as she walked to the casket to look at her husband's face for one final time. Daniel and Becky held hands tightly; all three children were watchful and disbelieving. Sophie bent over the casket. Tenderly she touched Boris's fingers folded piously over his chest. With the tolerance and understanding borne of many years of companionship, she fulfilled her promise to the dead man. She pressed into his clasped palms a personal check made out in the full amount of their hard-earned savings.

GA1328

You *Can* Take It with You

Point of View—Discussion Questions:

1. Did Sophie keep her promise to Boris, or did she break her promise? Remember that she wrote out a check in the full amount of their life savings.

   Possible Answer:

   Sophie kept her promise by leaving a check in the casket which represented the full amount of their life savings. Among the living, a check is regarded as a legitimate form of financial transaction. A check is a written order to a bank to pay the stated amount of money from one's bank account. Boris could spend the check, in death, as easily as he could spend cash money in death. Sophie promised to "honor" her husband's request. What is more—she gave comfort to a dying man who, for whatever reason, wanted to take his money with him to the grave.

2. Are there some kinds of promises which should be more binding than others—or is a promise a promise no matter what it involves? Expand on this.

3. Why does money cause conflict in families? How is it possible that both too much or not enough money can cause problems?

GA1328

You *Can* Take It with You

Improvisation—Role-Play Variations:

1. Play the deathbed scene or any other scene with dramatic possibilities which helps to amplify some of the issues in the story.

2. In several groups, work on skits entitled "But You Promised!" Present a variety of episodes that will demonstrate reasons for breaking promises. The choice may be from the serious to the sublime. Which promises would be the most forgivable to break (if any)? Consider parents and their promises to their children.

3. Select two opposing teams to present persuasive speeches on
   - "Money Brings Trouble"
   - "Money Brings Responsibility"

Speakers should try to convince the audience to accept their team's point of view. Discuss any issues that were presented by any of the team members which were significant.

"YOU PROMISED!"

You *Can* Take It with You

Writing Suggestions:

1. What is so important about a promise between family members, friends, or associates? State the reasons for your point of view. Based upon your opinion, do you believe that Sophie's actions were honorable or dishonorable?

2. In Mark Twain's *Adventures of Tom Sawyer*, there is a different approach to the topic of promises. "To promise *not* to do a thing is the surest way in the world to make a body want to go out and do that very thing." In a paragraph write an explanation of this from your own personal experience.

3. The U.S. government has economic statisticians working with the Bureau of the Census who produce information about household income distribution. As of 1989 a family of four that made less than $12,091 was considered to be living below the poverty level. In a newspaper article in *The Detroit Free Press* the journalist wrote, "But being poor and feeling poor are two different things."* Explain that point of view. Would a rich person or a poor person make that statement? How did you arrive at your answer?

---

*Ellen Creager, "Some People Are Rich in Spirit," *The Detroit Free Press*, February 2, 1990, Section F, p. 1.

GA1328

Chapter 2
You *Can* Take It with You
A Promise Is a Bond Sanctified by Trust
Student Comment

Characters: Boris, father   Daniel, middle son
            Sophie, mother   Becky, little sister
            Leon, oldest son

. . . .

In a paragraph express your feelings about any aspect of this story which you liked or disliked. How would you have changed it?

Alternative: Now that the story has been discussed, explain the proverb above from your point of view.

. . . .

_____

_____

_____

_____

_____

_____

_____

_____

_____

_____

_____

_____

_____

_____

_____

_____

_____

_____

Chapter 3
Sand Art, on Deadline

Chapter 3
Sand Art, on Deadline
Synopsis

Mike Angelo, a sculptor, goes to the seashore with all his sculpting equipment and over a period of several hours begins to build a majestic castle of sand. The passing crowd is drawn by the power of his talent as he creates medieval doorways flanked by U-shaped towers, elaborate systems of bridges and gates, battlements, and spiral staircases. The beach people begin to form a large appreciative audience who are captured by the romance of his work. When Angelo completes the last refinements on this miniaturized masterpiece, the crowd is enthralled and then dumbfounded by what follows.

GA1328

Chapter 3
Sand Art, on Deadline*

Talent Is a Divine Gift—Not to Be Squandered

Anonymous

The young man arrived on the Massachusetts beach early carrying a portable radio, a shovel, and an odd assortment of tools. There were a bricklayer's trowel, a palette knife, spatulas, spoons, and a spray bottle.

He walked down near the water—the tide was out—put down the radio and tuned it to soft rock. Then he shoveled wet sand into a pile nearly four feet high and as many feet across. He took up the trowel and used it to slice large hunks off the pile, creating a rectangular shape.

After that, he set to work with palette knife, spatulas, and spoons. He shaped a graceful tower, topped walls with crenelated battlements, fashioned elegant bay windows, and carved out a massive front gate.

The man knew his sand. With deft strokes, he smoothly finished some surfaces, embroidered baroque designs on others. As delicate shapes began to dry, he gently moistened them with water from the spray bottle, lest they crumble in the breeze.

---

*Copyright 1989 by The New York Times Company. Reprinted by permission. Sunday, August 13, 1989, Section 22E.

GA1328

All this took hours. People gathered, commenting to each other and asking questions of the sculptor. Lost in concentration, he gave only perfunctory replies. At last he stood back, apparently satisfied with a castle worthy of the Austrian countryside or Disneyland.

Then he gathered his tools and radio and moved them up to drier sand. He had known for a while what many in the rapt crowd still overlooked; the tide was coming in. Not only had he practiced his craft with confidence and style, he had done so against a powerful, immutable deadline.

24

GA1328

As the spectators looked on, water began to lap at the base of the castle. In minutes it was surrounded, a miniature Mont-Saint-Michel. Then the rising flood began to erode the base, chunks of wall fell, the tower tumbled, finally the gate's arch collapsed. More minutes passed, and small waves erased bay windows and battlements—soon no more than a modest lump was left.

Many in the crowd looked distraught; some voiced dismay. But the sculptor remained serene. He had, after all, had a wonderful day, making beauty out of nothing, and watching it return to nothing as time and tide moved on.

GA1328

Sand Art, on Deadline

For the Teacher:

Here is another twist to the end of the sand castle story which demonstrates that not all people who build castles in the sand are drifters, dreamers, or leisure time artisans!

In California there is a unique enterprise which sells sand sculpting, to order. The castles (and other scenes) are constructed to be used as a promotional lure to attract crowds to shopping malls, conventions, and special events of all kinds. The structures, further described in the brochure of *Sand Sculptors International*, are remarkable in their grandeur and accuracy:

> "Todd Vander Pluym and his SSI staff are not only the current U.S. Open, World, and International Sand Sculpture Champions, but they also hold all current world records for sand sculpture. SSI artisans, supervised by Todd, have been creating sand sculpture for more than 40 years. Todd is an architect by training, an artist by design and a sculptor by desire. He holds more than 160 sand sculpture championships including 4 world championships and 6 U.S. Open championships."

Sand sculpture is described in this literature as "The Ultimate Promotion." And so we have a double twist on a story when we are later informed that building things out of sand has been turned into a profit-making business by some people with extraordinary vision and enterprise. As immigrants to our shores would say, "Only in America!"

Sand Art, on Deadline

Point of View—Discussion Questions:

1. Why would a talented person such as Mike Angelo, the sculptor, put hard work into a creative project and be willing to see it disappear or be destroyed irretrievably by time and the elements?

Possible Answer:

Perhaps Mike Angelo, the artist, had hardly been able to sell his art, and the financial return was not worth the cost of his materials. But more importantly he realized that his greatest fulfillment was in the genuine pleasure he experienced in the process of making his sculpture. His castle was an expression of his talent and his interest in working with sand as a medium. This fact was more important to him than profit or recognition.

2. Some people think that creative women and men in the arts have a gift which they should share with others. First, they believe that those with talent have an obligation to the future. Secondly, they believe that the work of such artists should be created to endure as part of human history and as a chronicle of the times. Another point of view holds that talent belongs to the fortunate few, and it is theirs to use as they please. If some artists choose to create works that do not last for future enjoyment, there are those who believe that is the artist's decision and no one else's business. What do you believe?

3. What would the world be like if nothing was handed down in the arts, the sciences, or in technology? How would it be to reinvent the wheel with every new generation? What are the implications of having no previous information to draw on from the past? What do our achievements owe to the past in all fields of endeavor?*

4. Theodore Dreiser, an American novelist (1871-1945), described the arts as "The stored honey of the human soul, gathered on wings . . . ." How would you explain that quote?

---

*The oldest (1909) not-for-profit arts service organization in the U.S. organizes and circulates art exhibitions which travel to cultural institutions all over the country. Their mission is to foster art appreciation nationally. For more information write to: The American Federation of Arts, Public Information Officer, 41 East 65th St., New York 10021.

GA1328

Sand Art, on Deadline

Improvisation—Role-Play Variations:

1. Role-play the sand castle event on the beach from the standpoint of four or five observers and a narrator as if it were a sporting event. Improvise a running commentary describing the audience, the scene, and the construction of this magnificent structure.

2. As a TV newscaster, interview some of the observers at the seashore who were shocked when the tide came in and gouged out huge chunks of Mike Angelo's stunning work. Some people know Mike from "around" and have strong views on his art and his personality. Some think he's a genius; others say he's just a beach bum with an oversized ego. There is a group who believe that anyone who puts in so much effort for nothing must be a little crazy.

3. Conduct a committee meeting of the National Endowment for the Arts. Your group has funds to appropriate to worthy artists in your community of Anytown. There are different points of view among the members regarding the worthiness of certain works of art and disagreement about which artists deserve some support for their creative endeavors. Some of you like representational art and consider modern art as junk. Others dislike traditional art but strongly prefer works with a modern perspective. Express your standards for awarding grant money. Will you be big enough to give grant money to someone with talent whose work you find to be disagreeable? Express the problems as you go along. What qualifies people to be on a committee which has the power to give out grant money from taxes? Should the committee members be experts on art or be watchdogs for the taxpayers?

GA1328

Sand Art, on Deadline

Writing Suggestions:

1. If, at this time, you could be an accomplished musician, artist, singer, sports figure, dancer, writer, or scientist, what would you choose to be and how important would it be to you to win the recognition and applause of the public? Would personal satisfaction be enough? Explain your attitude.

2. Yesterday you read in the newspaper that in November, 1987, a painting by Vincent Van Gogh entitled *Irises* was sold at Sothebey's auction establishment in London, England, for $54 million dollars. The picture was not bought by an art lover but was bought as an investment. You know that the artist, Van Gogh, died sick and in poverty! Write a letter to the man who bought the picture. What is your reaction to the purchase and what would you say? Express your outrage, or dismay, or your admiration for the purchaser's keen business sense. How would the artist, Van Gogh, feel if he were to come back from the grave and hear about this purchase?

3. All art and folk art does not hang in museums. Included in this rich category are the comics which are a serious part of American mythology and a unique artistic expression. There is a highly individualized style to the characters and a special language that is demonstrated through the dialogue balloons. The art, the characterization, and the dialogue combine to impart a strong impression on the reader. Bring in your favorite comic strip and describe the qualities that you believe make it an effective artistic expression. (For some interesting insights, read *My Life in the Comics* by Will Eisner).

GA1328

Chapter 3
Sand Art, on Deadline
Talent Is a Divine Gift—Not to Be Squandered
Student Comment

Characters: Mike Angelo, artist
TV newscaster
Audience at the beach

· ·

In a paragraph express your feelings about any aspect of this story which you liked or disliked. How would you have changed it?

Alternative: Now that the story has been discussed, explain the proverb above from your point of view.

· ·

_____

_____

_____

_____

_____

_____

_____

_____

_____

_____

_____

_____

_____

_____

_____

_____

_____

GA1328

Chapter 4
The Blanket

GA1328

Chapter 4
The Blanket*

Synopsis

Brendan O'Brien and his wife, Katy, are Irish tenant farmers who live with their little boy Sean and with Grampa who is dearly loved by his grandson. Because they are desperately poor, Sean's mother and father are always searching for ways to survive their impoverished existence. One day Brendan and Katy decide upon a solution which seems hard-hearted and unconscionable. Just as they are about to act on this plan, their son, Sean, makes a suggestion that has shattering implications for their own future.

*Retold by Greta B. Lipson, Ed.D., from *Favorite Folktales from Around the World*, edited by Jane Yolen (New York: Random House, 1986).

GA1328

Chapter 4
The Blanket

We Reap as We Have Sown

Retold by Greta B. Lipson

Perhaps there were other poor people in the county, but none of the tenant farmers were poorer than Brendan O'Brien and his wife, Katy. Their young son, Sean, was a happy child, oblivious to the hardships and the grinding poverty suffered by his parents and his grandfather. He was always at play—curious and acutely alert to everything around him on the farm.

Every day was an experience of discovery for Sean and his questions never stopped. But the O'Brien's were far too worn out at the end of the day from working their small farm to have any patience left for the little boy. Besides—there were real problems that compounded their constant struggle. Brendan reminded his wife, "The rent is due soon, Katy, and we've put very little by to pay the landlord."

"Too many mouths to feed here," she grumbled in response.

GA1328

Only Grampa had the patience to answer Sean's questions. The old man had lived with them since Sean was an infant, working the farm side by side with the young family. Finally age had bent his bones and he was not strong enough to keep up the hard labor. But none of this mattered to Sean, who only cared that his grampa was his very best companion. For every question Sean asked, the old man had an answer embedded in an elaborate story. He told about Celtic tribes who came from the island of Great Britain, and he told about the Viking raiders who invaded the east and south coasts of Ireland.

34

GA1328

Then Grampa would spin a geography lesson and say, "There were the first towns of Ireland and they'd be Cork and Dublin, Limerick and Waterford . . . ." And Sean listened, loving their time together.

Slowly the joyous days began to wane and there filtered in a dismal overlay in the atmosphere of the small cottage. Sean grew aware of a mood of misery that surfaced with more arguments over the dinner table. It was the only time the small family sat down together, and the sound of the same ugly refrain was heard over and over again. He had heard it all before but he began to listen carefully to try to understand the cause.

"Too many mouths to feed in this house. If we could trim down the food and drink we might be able to save some money." Sean's mother, Katy, seemed to have a better understanding of expenses and management than his father. Clearly money was at the root of the problem.

As far as Sean could tell, his father, Brendan, resisted the litany of complaints that came from his mother. Brendan would only say, "But Katy—he's my very own father!" His brow would furrow and make a dark line that marked his face with brooding.

Through all of this the grandfather seemed not to hear. He grew quieter through the miserable winter days and nights. They talked around him as if he did not exist. There was no more telling of stories for Sean and sometimes at the table, when the surly exchange would begin between his parents, the boy noticed that something would come over Grampa's eyes—an opaque glaze—as if he were turned inward, listening to distant voices, perhaps kinder and more bearable. The old man's head was bowed more, and he would look down as if to study the food in his dinner bowl. When he finished eating, he was careful not to move until the others left the table. It was as if he did not wish to remind them that he was present in the room.

Then it happened on a day when they were all in the house huddled against the outside weather—sullen and silent. "Now is as good a time as any," Katy O'Brien told her husband. She was sharp and angry with him—but that is the way she was these days.

"Does it have to be today?" Brendan asked.

"This is as good a day as you'll get," she said—her voice rising, insistent, determined.

All at once Sean understood. The solution to their desperation would be to have one less mouth to feed. Grampa was to be turned out to fend for himself. Together, Brendan and Katy took the old man by his elbow, lifting him out of his chair. He was quiet as death. He did not protest. Somehow they had prepared him for this—their last act of filial responsibility, and he knew it was coming.

37

GA1328

Sean saw his grandfather being moved toward the door—a sleepwalker in a painful dream, about to be cast out into an uncertain future. Katy hesitated. She spoke. "Here, let's give him a blanket off the bed." Briskly—with no motion wasted—she turned toward the cot nearest the fireplace and swept the blanket off the bed. She wrapped it around his poor rounded shoulders—and made of him a pathetic bundle of a human being.

"Wait, Mother!" her little son shouted. "Just give him half a blanket, I beg of you."

"But why?" his parents asked in shocked surprise over their son's interference.

"Please give Grampa half a blanket—then I will have something to give to you both when it's my time to turn you out."

GA1328

The Blanket

Point of View—Discussion Questions:

1. What values in our culture give this story its impact? What is there in the conclusion that is personally upsetting to some readers?

   Possible Answer:

   Our social code teaches us to honor our parents and to be responsible for those we love. The ending is disturbing because of the inhumanity of turning out an elderly and vulnerable human being. The profound effect is introduced by the little boy, Sean, who has witnessed the example his parents have set. His statement makes it clear that the same miserable fate of abandonment waits for his mother and father, and Sean will be the one to carry on this treachery against them. On a purely selfish level, the events suggest that the same thing could happen to any one of us when we are old and helpless.

2. In the context of this story, how do you explain this proverb: "What goes around comes around"? What evidence is there that this statement is true or false? How would justice be done if the proverb were true? Explain the following: "Be to your parents such a one as you would pray your children be to you." (Attributed to Isocrates, a great Greek orator 436-338 B.C.)

3. Given the poverty and desperation of Brendan and Katy O'Brien, what other course of action could they have followed to solve their money problems? What realistic advice could you give to these poor Irish tenant farmers? Is it true that some human problems have no solutions?

GA1328

The Blanket

Improvisation—Role-Play Variations:

1. Play the scene in the home of Brendan and Katy O'Brien, just as it reads, when Grampa is about to be turned out of the house. Extend the dialogue between Sean and his parents to whatever point the actors choose. Mr. and Mrs. O'Brien believe they are doing the only thing they can to help them survive.

2. Grampa and his grandson, Sean, discuss a plan to run away together. They try to analyze the difficulties of supporting themselves and explore the possibilities of an old man and a child earning enough money to survive. They are motivated by their companionship and love for one another.

3. The old man discovers the plan to turn him out. He prefers to retain his dignity and leave the O'Brien household voluntarily. In time Grampa becomes a beloved and financially successful storyteller who travels over the entire country. Brendan and Katy arrange a meeting with him. He agrees but is certain that they are in financial need and that is their only reason for having communicated with him. What happens at the meeting?

GA1328

The Blanket

Writing Suggestions:

1. Write a paragraph describing specific ways in which senior citizens are able to help young people. Think about schools, community centers, hospitals, and places of business. Research grandparent surrogate programs. What important function do such programs provide for adults and young people alike?

2. The Social Security system in our country is the only source of income for many retired old people. Research the details of this program and explain its benefits in a paragraph. All American citizens are affected by this program in which we all have a Social Security number. From what you understand, how much are these monthly payments and is the amount enough to live on currently? How does a senior citizen survive who has no family, no support system, and can no longer earn a living?*

3. There is a large organization called The American Association of Retired Persons (AARP) which publishes a magazine called *Modern Maturity*. Find a copy in your local public library and review its contents. List the issues in which older citizens are interested. What are their political and social concerns? Why should this make any difference to you?

4. Describe an older member of your family or someone who is a family friend. If you project into the future, what kind of an old person do you imagine you will be? What do you hope to do in your advanced years?

*For *An Introduction to Social Security* Booklet Code No. 514 W, write to Consumer Information Center-P, Box 100, Pueblo, Colorado 81002.

GA1328

Chapter 4
The Blanket
We Reap as We Have Sown
Student Comment

Characters: Sean, the little boy
Brendan and Katy O'Brien, his parents
Grampa

. . . .

In a paragraph express your feelings about any aspect of this story which you liked or disliked. How would you have changed it?

Alternative: Now that the story has been discussed, explain the proverb above from your point of view.

. . . .

_____

_____

_____

_____

_____

_____

_____

_____

_____

_____

_____

_____

_____

_____

_____

_____

_____

_____

GA1328

Chapter 5
Mrs. Esposito's Pizza

Chapter 5
Mrs. Esposito's Pizza
Synopsis

Victor is a rich dude with gold chains, sharp clothes and all the outward signs of financial success. He has clearly overcome his poor beginnings as he wheels his big car back to his old slum neighborhood to buy one of Mrs. Esposito's pizzas. Swaggering into the restaurant, he gives his careful order, all the while happy and high spirited with the prospect of his luscious supper. Victor leaves the store with a big steaming pizza in hand. The unexpected turn of events leaves Victor half dead with fright and bewilderment!

GA1328

Chapter 5
Mrs. Esposito's Pizza

Things Are Seldom What They Seem

By Greta B. Lipson

Victor was always comfortable going back to his old neighborhood. He never made it a secret that he grew up there—indeed it was his badge of honor. In no way was he ashamed of his humble beginnings nor was he embarrassed about his determined trip out of the place. As a matter of fact he now felt inordinate pride over his present status. He loved being rich and successful.

Victor couldn't explain it, but there was always this need to go back to the streets of his youth. Perhaps it reaffirmed his authenticity and made him a better person—one whose affluence had not spoiled him. Victor was fond of saying, "You can take the boy out of the slum, but you can't take the slum out of the boy!"

The familiar sights were reassuring to him. Of course there were some changes over the years—but many of the store fronts were just as he remembered them. He relished the pungent smells, the ragtag people, the jumbled merchandise, the sounds and the spicy ethnic treats! Unlike the way he lived as a deprived child, he was now able to buy absolutely anything that appealed to his palate. That fact of life was a lasting joy to his stomach. No more unfulfilled yearning for him! He could afford to have it all.

The daily newspaper had made a big thing about developers who were gentrifying the neighborhood—making it more attractive for the young professionals who were moving in. But he wasn't worried about any serious inroads into the look and feel of the place. The new residents would surely consider it important to protect the old "flavor" of the streets and the shops. They would glory in its vintage, and it would forever be his old neighborhood.

Easing his Mercedes against the curb in a clearly marked "No Parking" zone, Victor began to review mentally the tasty choices which would appear on the menu over the backboard. Double pepperoni? Absolutely! Anchovies? Too salty—but they made the thirst-quenching soda pop so acutely delicious. Olives? You said it! He imagined black olives looking up at him like cartoon circles unblinking in a sea of bubbly aromatic tomato sauce. As usual his choice would be an Esposito's Special. His stomach was sending messages to his brain which was generating even more fantasies. He rehearsed the very first slice of pizza—cut adrift in space—separated from its crispy moorings. He envisioned warm attenuated strings of mozzarella cheese hanging on—then disengaged—finally finding their way up to his eager lips.

46

It always happened this way, and it never ceased to amaze him that thoughts of food could cause a rush of saliva. He was like one of Pavlov's psychologically conditioned dogs. All it took was one thought of the pizza, and a great surge of saliva filled his mouth in readiness for the feast.

Once inside Esposito's, he gave the deliberate order of an aficionado and hung over the counter longingly. He would play a time game with himself while he waited patiently for the oven to give up its wondrous baked delight. Finally the pizza was pulled from the hearth, was lovingly dusted with hot peppers, and was packaged. Victor smelled that fragrance which was at once a mix of an oregano cloud and a hot cardboard box.

Almost at the very moment he stepped out of the store he felt a presence behind him. "Stop right there, Bozo, and don't even think about turning around!" He clutched his outsize pizza box as if he were a rigid sentry standing watch.

GA1328

Victor felt an insistent, unmistakable object thrust painfully into his ribs. A gun. Somebody was actually holding him up in front of a busy pizza joint. Where was everybody at supper time anyway? He had heard stories about the physical sensations people experienced when in a state of fright. Can you really vomit on an empty stomach, he wondered? He repressed a whimper but was horrified when a pathetic sound escaped.

"Whaja say?" His assailant was anxious. Then, not waiting for an answer, the guy with the gun threatened, "Just shuddup, Bozo."

A beseeching voice came out of Victor's throat. "You can take anything I've got," he ventured. Was that piping voice actually his? He couldn't control it as it rambled on.

The snickered response was predictable. "Don't need no lip from you, Bozo."

Victor quickly inventoried the worldly goods on his body: a Count Dulane leather coat, a serpentine gold chain around his neck, a diamond initial ring, and his brand-new imported watch. That watch was his baby, his status symbol. Its weight pressed heavily—conspicuously as it glimmered on his wrist. He clung to the pizza as a toddler to its blanket—the warmth of it heating his numbed belly.

GA1328

The rest happened quickly. With a dancer's grace the mugger pulled the gun out of Victor's ribs, did an astonishing pirouette, whirled in front of him and looked into Victor's eyes, full face. With one brutal wrench, the thug tore at Victor's frozen hands, whipped his wrists and pulled away his prize. He took off down the street at breakneck speed with coattails flying—like a western duster on a frontier bad guy. The hapless Victor watched, disbelieving, as the hoodlum disappeared from sight like a phantom streak.

49

GA1328

Shaken almost insensible from fright, Victor lurched in a half faint, dropping to the pavement on one knee. The curb broke his fall and gave him meager comfort as he sat with his head buried in his arms. He sobbed uncontrollably. "Oh thank you, thank you, God!" he slobbered, "I can't believe it! I'm still alive. That idiot left everything I had worth stealing, and all he took was my pizza!"

GA1328

Mrs. Esposito's Pizza

Point of View—Discussion Questions:

1. Is the mugger less a thief for having stolen a pizza worth a few dollars instead of robbing Victor of his watch or gold chain which were worth a fortune?

   Possible Answer:
   The legal definiton of *larceny* means "taking away someone else's property unlawfully with the intention of permanently depriving the owner of its use." The legal definition of *robbery* means "taking property from a person by force or fear." Either way, the law regards the theft of the pizza as a crime. However, a judge or a prosecutor or a jury would probably take into account the value of the object taken.

2. A *misdemeanor* is defined as "a minor crime usually punishable by less than one year in jail and/or a fine." What factor is there in this incident that would make it more serious? (The use of a gun makes this a crime of armed robbery, which is a felony. The law considers crimes of violence against people more serious than crimes against property.)

3. Why do you think someone would risk the possible penalty of armed robbery, if convicted, just to grab something to eat? What is the reason that people commit crimes in general? Statistics indicate that more crimes are committed by young people than by older people. What would you say are the reasons for this?

4. Where would you go if you were homeless and needed a meal to keep body and soul together? Are there soup kitchens and shelters available in your city to feed and house children and adults who are homeless? Who sponsors and supports these places?

Mrs. Esposito's Pizza

Improvisation—Role-Play Variations:

1. A television reporter has been alerted by a "Neighborhood Watch" group about Victor's mugging. The reporter is on the scene and is interviewing the owner of the pizza parlor, Mrs. Esposito, and others. The neighbors express strong feelings about Victor, whom they regard as a show-off who was asking for trouble. Mrs. Esposito disagrees with them vigorously and is very vocal about it.

2. The mugger has been apprehended and is at the police station. An attorney, Mr. Loophole, has been appointed by the court to represent him. They are in a private room discussing the mugger's defense. What is he telling the attorney about his motives and what actually occurred? How could you make him a sympathetic character despite the charges against him?

3. An argument occurs in the old neighborhood among the residents regarding Victor and his attitudes. Some claim that Victor doesn't have a social conscience because he turned his back on them and their problems and moved away. Since he acquired money he has no interest whatever in their difficulties. The neighbors claim that if he cared about them he would be involved constructively in the community. Victor replies by saying that moving upward and out is what America is all about. He thinks they are all unfair.

GA1328

Mrs. Esposito's Pizza

Writing Suggestions:

1. Describe something upsetting that has happened to you. How could you have avoided the incident by making other choices or decisions about your actions? If you had no control over what happened, did the event occur because you were in the wrong place at the wrong time? Did poor judgment or fate play a role in the happening?

2. What personal possessions do you value which have great meaning to you but would have little or no monetary value to anyone else? Explain the sentiment that is involved with this item.

3. Based upon the characterization of Victor in the story, what was your impression of the kind of person he was? Did your attitude toward him affect your feelings about him as a victim? Write a statement.

4. Do you believe it is wrong or offensive to display the trappings of wealth? Or was Victor just plain stupid? What circumstances would influence your decision in any situation in regard to how you would dress or act?

GA1328

Chapter 5
Mrs. Esposito's Pizza
Things Are Seldom What They Seem
Student Comment

Characters: Victor
                 A mugger
                 Mrs. Esposito, restaurant owner
                 Neighbors

. . . .

In a paragraph express your feelings about any aspect of this story which you liked or disliked. How would you have changed it?

Alternative: Now that the story has been discussed, explain the proverb above from your point of view.

. . . .

Chapter 6
Bon Appetit

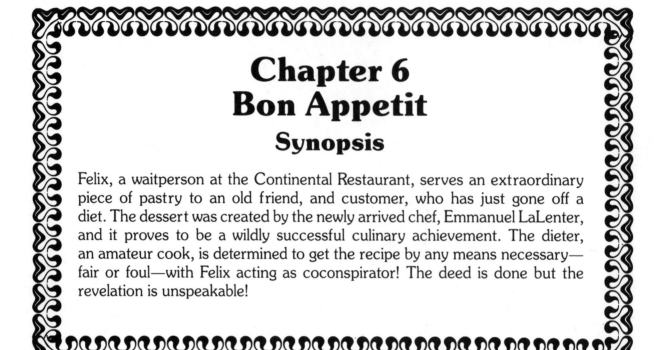

Chapter 6
Bon Appetit
Synopsis

Felix, a waitperson at the Continental Restaurant, serves an extraordinary piece of pastry to an old friend, and customer, who has just gone off a diet. The dessert was created by the newly arrived chef, Emmanuel LaLenter, and it proves to be a wildly successful culinary achievement. The dieter, an amateur cook, is determined to get the recipe by any means necessary— fair or foul—with Felix acting as coconspirator! The deed is done but the revelation is unspeakable!

GA1328

Chapter 6
Bon Appetit

What You Don't Know Won't Hurt You

By Greta B. Lipson

I'm not one of those selfish, secretive people who refuses to share a recipe—but I worked so hard to get this one and risked so much that I'm not sure the goddess of cooking and baking would allow me to hand it out.

It all happened a few weeks ago, when I had just gone off one of my many diets and felt that I deserved a treat worthy of my good behavior. After all those painful months of deprivation—right or wrong—I was determined to make this a reward to remember. My friends don't call me "El-Blimpo" for nothing. But the truth is that I would rather starve for two days and then splurge my calories on a gastronomic joy than eat a barnful of bran and a bale of hay because it's good for me.

The word on the street was that there was a new chef at the Continental who made pastries one could die for! His name was Emmanuel LaLenter, and he was everything one would expect from a world-class chef, which translated means he was arrogant, temperamental, and impossible to get along with. But how those customers slavered over his creations. The patrons were extravagant with praise.

GA1328

I, too, was one of those manic customers dying to try LaLenter's delights, and I showed up at the Continental Restaurant as soon as I could get there. Felix, the waitperson, knew me as a steady customer with a fatal weakness for desserts. Besides that he understood that I was an adventuresome amateur cook who loved to turn out luscious dishes to feed to my friends. When I sat down, Felix came over in a flash. We were good old buddies, and he knew I was there because my penance was over.

"You heard already, right?" He smiled his best smile reserved only for the people who understood really fine food. We were kindred souls. Felix served excellent cuisine with pride, and I obliged by eating it with passion!

"I'm not here for dinner, Felix. I'm here with a clean and highly tuned palate for just one single dish that this LaLenter fellow makes. In your experienced and wise judgment, what is his foremost achievement in pastry?"

He warmed to my question and, looking upward, seemed to be searching for the answer on the ceiling. I knew better than to make smart remarks at a time like this. He was giving my question serious consideration and was to be respected! I was silent and patient. He finally responded, "My recommendation to you for a first adventure is LaLenter's Black Satin Pie paved with chantilly cream."

"Are you suggesting something as homely as pie? All-American pie? Not 'haute cuisine'?" I asked timidly.

Felix didn't take kindly to my reaction, "Don't insult me. Would I steer you wrong? Have I ever disappointed you?"

Everything was in readiness: the fine china, the damask napkin, the single rose in the bud vase, a carafe of aromatic coffee, and a chilled dessert fork. I sat expectantly, like a greedy child. Felix set the wedge of Black Satin Pie in front of me. Oh joy and perfection. The presentation was glorious and uncluttered. Only a single strawberry dipped in white chocolate sat at the side of the plate. A perky green stem poked out through the swirls of chocolate.

Black Satin was an implosion on my palate, all gloriously creamy in a bittersweet chocolate triumph. I felt my eyelids flutter in the ecstasy of the moment. The nutlike crust was sinfully delicate, unlike anything I had ever experienced before. Filling and crust were wedded in a swooning combination made richer by the billowing chantilly cream—sweetened with a subtle, aromatic orange honey. The eating was slow. When I was finished I sat, as if in a reverie, looking at the empty plate.

Whatever I had to do to unlock the recipe of Black Satin Pie—I was prepared to do. Felix was my only hope. Remember that he talks the language of good food, but he is not interested in creating it. To want to produce a culinary creation in one's own kitchen, you must be moved by a compelling lust to cook. What is more, you must enjoy listening to the admiring approval from your eaters who make subvocal, primitive sounds meaning "I have fallen madly in love with your food!"

I cajoled and threatened Felix and in a challenging test of our friendship, he copied the secret recipe from LaLenter's private file. I was thrilled—but there was one more very serious obstacle for me. How in the world did he make that heavenly flaky pastry with its intricate scalloped edge?

Felix couldn't find any evidence of the recipe in the file. "But I do have a suggestion," he said, warming to the task. "Why don't you pretend that you are going to use the phone next to the back door of the kitchen? The door there has a perfect porthole window to watch through. LaLenter's pastry table is right by the door, and you'll have a good view of everything he does. Make sure you come in the late morning when the deliveries are over. That's just about the time he gets started on his fancy baking. And for heaven's sake, watch out for his assistant, Big Jenny. She watches over him protectively, like a bear with a cub. Have no doubt that she would probably kill you if she knew what you were up to!"

61

GA1328

The hallway was dark near the kitchen door and I was there, slightly scared because I could hear Big Jenny hollering orders to the staff. My eyes grew accustomed to the dim light, and I watched as LaLenter prepared his nine-inch (22.86 cm) pie plates for the pastry. The pie shells were made from a water-whisk recipe which I had never seen before, but I was more interested in the cute, kinky crimped edge he designed at the rim of the crust. He rolled out the dough expertly. As I watched him, I went through the steps in my mind. Easy now. Tear the waxed paper off the circle of dough. Dampen the rim of the pan so the shell won't shrink while it bakes. Fit it gently into the pie pan and now—start crimping the edge.

GA1328

LaLenter didn't lose a motion as he pulled his big, ugly false teeth out of his mouth. I believe they were his uppers—plastic pink gums and all. At first I didn't understand what was happening. He didn't wipe the teeth off on his apron or anything. Instead he held them against the outside of the rim of dough on the pie pan. He pressed those fake choppers against the dough methodically and proceeded to push his thumb hard against the dough. The result was the cunning little pattern traced into the scalloped edge of the Black Satin piecrust that I had admired so much.

Fighting waves of nausea, I hung around just long enough to confirm that LaLenter trimmed all the pastry crusts in the same way. When he was through with his last creation, he popped those disgusting, discolored teeth back into his slack mouth like a demented genius. As for me—I was seriously sick for the rest of the day.

Bon Appetit

For the Teacher:

This is a true story and therefore to be honest with my readers, I have decided to include the recipe for Black Satin Pie.

Black Satin Pie

Bake a nine-inch (22.86 cm) pie shell.*

Before starting, warm 4 egg whites to room temperature in a separate bowl. Set yolks aside.

Melt together in a microwave oven or in a double boiler
  1 six-ounce (177.44 ml) package semisweet chocolate pieces
  2 tablespoons (30 ml) sugar
  3 tablespoons (45 ml) milk
Blend together and cool.
Beat into cooled mixture, one at a time
  4 egg yolks
  1 teaspoon (5 ml) vanilla

Beat egg white until stiff. Fold into chocolate mixture. Pour into baked, cooled pie shell. Refrigerate for an hour; then add topping.

Cover with a chantilly topping by adding 2 tablespoons (30 ml) of honey or 2 tablespoons (30 ml) of orange marmalade to 1 cup (240 ml) of whipping cream or instead, add 1-3 tablespoons (15-45 ml) of confectioners' sugar. (You may prefer to use prepared whipped topping.) The pie is best when refrigerated for twenty-four hours.

---

*The original pie crust recipe is divine but difficult to work with. Your own baked crust will be just fine. But if your curiosity moves you, send a self-addressed, stamped business envelope to me, G. Lipson, at P.O. Box 3452, Ann Arbor, MI 48106, and I'll send you the recipe for the water-whisk crust.

GA1328

Bon Appetit

Point of View—Discussion Questions:

1. What would your local Board of Health think of the notion that "What you don't know won't hurt you"?

   Possible Answer:
   The Board of Health is concerned with problems of public health in order to prevent and control the spread of disease. Communities are concerned with sanitation, contagious disease, immunization, animal bites, and other factors relative to the public well-being. Health codes and laws on local, state, and national levels are enforced to protect the population. Because the Board of Health does its utmost to educate and inform the population about good health practices, its philosophy would be, "What you don't know *can* hurt you."

2. Every semester history professor Milton Covensky of Wayne State University in Detroit would lecture to his students on two of their favorite topics. How would you define and explain the following?

   - The Tragedy of Ignorance (having no information or understanding of social and natural forces and events in life and therefore having no control)
   - The Tragedy of Knowledge (understanding and recognizing social and natural forces in life and being powerless to change the course of events)
   - Which of the above would you rather have?

3. What would you do if reporting Chef LaLenter's unsanitary kitchen practices were to put Felix's job in jeopardy? If you report someone for having done something seriously wrong, what could the consequences be? How does your relationship to that person affect your decision? Is there ever another way of dealing with a sticky situation aside from reporting it to the authorities? (Think about school situations.)

GA1328

Bon Appetit

Improvisation—Role-Play Variations:

1. Pantomime the entire restaurant scene, as it reads, with the patron in ecstasy over the wonderful dessert. He wants to compliment everybody effusively—most especially Felix, the waitperson, and Emmanuel LaLenter, the pastry chef!

2. Pantomime the entire restaurant scene, with a difficult patron who is incredibly dissatisified with the service, the dessert, and almost everything. After a confrontation with the management and the help, the unhappy customer storms out of the restaurant!

3. Assume the role of a Board of Health inspector assigned to Dirty Gertie's Homestyle Grill. With your clipboard in hand and Gertie at your elbow, how many and what kind of infractions do you encounter? Use your common sense as you discover one violation after another and complain out loud to Gertie about what you have found. Your disgust is obvious.

Bon Appetit

Writing Suggestions:

1. Suppose that you were a consumer who had a complaint about a food product that was misrepresented in the advertisement. You are annoyed enough to write a letter of complaint to the manufacturer. Be specific and convincing with your disappointment in their product. How would you want them to improve on it, or do you want a refund?

2. Recall a delightful or a yucky experience you have had with strange food. Perhaps you ate an exotic dish and later discovered it was minced tongue, squid, sweetbread, or stuffed intestine. Where were you and how did it happen that you were eating something unfamiliar? Include the details.

3. How can food processors or manufacturers mislead the public? What would the motive be? Write a statement with your opinion. (Following this lead, do some research on the famous book, *The Jungle,* by Upton Sinclair, written in 1906. The book created a sensation because it exposed shocking conditions in the meat-packing industry. This information attracted the attention of President Theodore Roosevelt, who invited the author to the White House. The story generated public outrage and led to the passage of the Pure Food and Drug Act. What did the book reveal?)

GA1328

Chapter 6
Bon Appetit
What You Don't Know Won't Hurt You
Student Comment

Characters: The Dieter, a restaurant patron
　　　　　　　Felix, a waitperson
　　　　　　　Emmanuel LaLenter, the chef

. . . .

In a paragraph express your feelings about any aspect of this story which you liked or disliked. How would you have changed it?

Alternative: Now that the story has been discussed, explain the proverb above from your point of view.

. . . .

_____

_____

_____

_____

_____

_____

_____

_____

_____

_____

_____

_____

_____

_____

_____

_____

_____

_____

Chapter 7
A Picture Is Worth a Thousand Words

Chapter 7
A Picture Is Worth a Thousand Words
Synopsis

Grandmother Iris Leica tells her grandchild, Nelly Nikon, that pictures record the absolute, irrefutable truth and are not corrupted by the bias of the written word. Inspired by the *purity* of her grandmother's convictions, Nelly becomes a child camera nut. She grows up to be a career photojournalist, proud of the integrity of her work. In her late professional experience she attends a seminar on new age cameras and learns about an advanced editing technology in photography which poses a great ethical danger. The far-reaching implications now make a mockery of Grandma Leica's convictions about truth in photography.

Chapter 7
A Picture Is Worth a Thousand Words

The Camera Captures a Moment of Truth

By Greta B. Lipson

"You can't always believe what you read, my dear child, but photographs are different." My grandmother, Iris Leica, was a woman with very strong convictions! "Look here, Nelly," she would say, shoving the daily newspaper under my nose. "You are seeing this with your very own eyes. Jake's store over in Bethany Beach was burning to the ground and the fire company with old poor equipment was battling with all its heart to control it. The camera doesn't lie! It's a powerful picture and packs a real wallop, without a whole lot of opinionated hot air from anybody!"

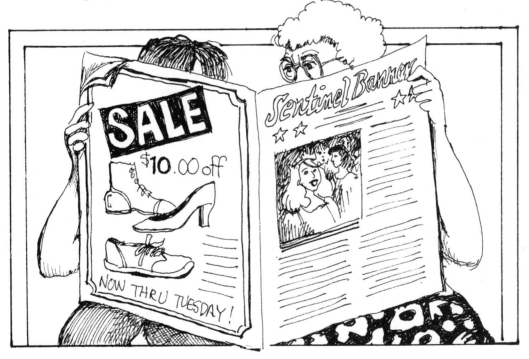

We would both pore over the daily edition of the *Sentinel Banner* with its wonderful photojournalism by Herbie Trueblue, whose name appeared under each picture. Like any town, there was the usual reportage of good news and bad news faithfully captured by reporters. Grandma often suspected reporters of being full of bias and baloney, but she trusted Herbie's pictures. He just took his pictures and the truth was revealed.

I hated to disagree with her, mainly because I usually lost, but I had to say it. "You know that stuff about honesty and pictures? What about all the times they leave things out of a picture, and you only know half of what's going on?"

GA1328

She shrugged her shoulders and didn't rise to my challenge, so I tried again. "How about when Mayor Snively was first elected and the newspaper pictures made him look like everybody's favorite uncle?"

"What's your point, short stuff?" Grandma knew how to needle me.

"Well . . . when there were suspicions that he was dipping into the city treasury and was really a crook, the photos in the newspaper changed. All of a sudden they made him look like a scum bag!"

"Oh well," she said, "same man, different angle."

"You're proving my point, Grandma!" She could be aggravating, but she was still great company.

My interest in photography probably started then, with Grandmother's blessings. By the time I was twelve I became an anointed truth-seeker known as "Nelly Nikon—The Camera Nut." I was spurred on by my passion for collecting images, limited only by the money I had to spend on equipment and film. Everybody and everything was my quarry. Nothing was safe from me and my camera, and that included anthills, ball games, garbage dumps, gophers coming out of holes and my friends, of course. Kids at school were the goofiest subjects because they usually couldn't think of anything better to do than stick out their tongues or stretch their mouths like chimps in the zoo! But I didn't care. They could stick out their tongues at the camera all they liked as long as I could snap them.

When I grew up, my love of photography didn't wane. My skill and interest developed into my profession. What could be better than doing what you love for a living? On one of my assignments I was invited to a seminar which advertised information on the astonishing advances of digital editing technology in photography. The audience was pretty sophisticated, I thought, and the woman who delivered the sales pitch was up to the challenge. I was glad to be there.

She started with the funny stuff—sort of sneaking up on us. The room was darkened and the slides appeared on the screen. Slide one: Here's the President of the United States addressing Congress wearing a clown suit! Slide two: Here's the Vice-President with a third eye and one enlarged ear. Laughter and some pungent political commentary went all around. Then things got serious. The salesperson moved her presentation from print media to TV to movies. The photographic altering, in every instance, was undiscernable to the eye. All kinds of astonishing changes had been made on the pictures and images before us, with no clue that outrageous tampering had taken place. It was an amazing yet disturbing demonstration.

Concern over the electronic capabilities of this new technology began to crowd out our wonderment. This was not the ordinary traditional editing that we knew so well. This was different. Clouds had been moved and skies made sunnier, a ravaged woodland was restored to look like a green paradise. In another instance, Egyptian pyramids had been rearranged to fit more conveniently on the cover of *National Geographic*.

GA1328

But then dangerous possibilities began to surface in our minds. What if a terrorist group were to broadcast pictures of a nuclear attack or some other disaster that had never occurred? What if a make-believe news commentator were to deliver a bulletin with simulated news shots about a revolution that had never taken place?

The dazzled members of the audience were asking rapid-fire questions about the mechanics of this new photographic technology. Finally one serious-looking man spoke up, "You haven't said anything about the enormous possibility for abuses of this technology. What about journalistic ethics?

"What about them?" the saleswoman shot back.

"Well," Mr. Serious said, "You've just shown us perfect pictures of things that didn't really happen. You've even told us about a machine that works with a microchip. That means there is no existing negative or original proof of what was actually photographed by a camera. You call that honest?" The entire audience was aware of being re-routed. They were quiet—waiting for an answer.

The saleswoman was clearly irritated now. A slightly disdainful edge crept into her voice. "Machines are not ethical or unethical, sir—people are!"

My heart sank as I listened to that exchange—I reflected to myself how life had changed. So much that we thought to be true is no longer so. We used to say, with so much conviction, that a picture is worth a thousand words. But now—with the advantages of modern technology and real progress, we can honestly say that a picture is worth a thousand lies.*

"Faster than you can say, 'visual credibility gap,' the 1980's are becoming the last decade in which photos can be considered evidence of anything."
J.D. Lasica, *Sacramento Bee* Staff Writer, 1988

"The photograph as we know it, as a record of fact, may no longer exist in three or four years."
George Wedding, Director of Photography
Sacramento Bee Newspaper, 1988

---

*This story is based upon an article by J.D. Lasica, *Sacramento Bee*, Sacramento, California, October 9, 1988, Forum Section, p. 1 "A Picture's Worth 1000 Lies." New digital technology is challenging journalistic ethics.

A Picture Is Worth a Thousand Words

For the Teacher:

Photo helps to clear man; he heads back to school

Associated Press

BOSTON—A man who lost his college scholarship and his job after he was convicted of assaulting a police officer during an antiwar demonstration has cleared his name with a 20-year-old photograph.

The photo, taken by a newspaper photographer but not published until this week, shows Malcolm Emory with an armload of books at about the time police said that he had thrown a rock.

Emory, now 39, maintains he was wrongly convicted of the assault, which occurred during a protest at Northeastern University in 1970. He said he was not involved in the protest and had just left the library.

He never served time for the conviction, but he lost his scholarship, his job doing research for the Navy, which depended on security clearance, and his hope for a future as a physicist.

But this year, using a newspaper photograph taken at the protest, Emory got his conviction set aside and won a new trial. On Wednesday, the Suffolk County, Mass., district attorney's office said it would drop the case. And on Thursday, Northeastern University awarded Emory, who has spent most of the last 20 years as a welder, a full scholarship to complete the physics studies he began there in 1969.

"I'm very happy to have this solved," Emory said.

Arresting officer Vincent Logan maintains that Emory threw a rock at police. Emory said he was attacked by the officer after he left the library and decided to take a look at the protest.

Emory was arrested on a charge of assault and battery on a police officer. He was convicted on Logan's testimony and given a six-month suspended sentence and three years' probation.

"I really expected some sort of apology from Logan," Emory said. But after four or five years and nothing was forthcoming, I realized I had to get on with my life."

So after his probation ended, Emory worked in machine shops and shipyards. But while at the library five years ago, Emory found a front-page photograph in the *Boston Globe* that showed him surrounded by police in the midst of the demonstration. His books could not be seen in the photograph, but that eventually led to another that provided sufficient grounds for a new trial.

Logan still disputes Emory's story, saying he was careful to keep his eye on the person who threw the rock, which injured another officer standing near him.

"All I saw was blood splatter, and I keep my eye on the guy who throws the rock," he said.

He said the photograph of Emory holding books was taken after his arrest, but he doesn't know where the books came from.

Emory re-enrolled at Northeastern last fall and hopes to complete his bachelor's degree next year.

GA1328

A Picture Is Worth a Thousand Words

For the Teacher:

This illustration is a re-creation of the photograph taken in 1970 when Malcolm Emory, a student, was being arrested by police. He was charged with assault at the scene of an anti-war protest at Northeastern University in Boston. He claimed he was an innocent observer, on his way from the library, with his arms loaded down with books, and was physically unable to throw the rock which struck a police officer. The actual photograph, which was taken by a photographer with the *Boston Globe*, supported Emory's story but was not published until 20 years later. (The Detroit Free Press, saturday, May 26, 1990, pge 13A, p.a.s.—AP Laster 61615/Boston Globe 1990). For original photo write to *Globe* Photo Dept., Box 2378, Boston MA 02107-2378. Description: Malcomb Emory, Bob Dean.

GA1328

A Picture Is Worth a Thousand Words

Point of View—Discussion Questions:

1. Is it overreacting to think that the new technology in photography will be used to distort the truth? Why should we care?

   Possible Answer:
   No, it is not overreacting. Propaganda has always been a tool of governments and people in power. Persuasive techniques and deception have been used to sway public opinion since humans have lived together. And media falsehood is the favored tool of tyrants and repressive governments. This new technology is something that makes deception a slicker option. There have always been special interests willing to distort the truth for personal gain. As a safeguard, in a democratic society, we must maintain a high standard of truth and honesty in order to inform and protect our citizens in a free society.

2. How do the ethics of changing a photo differ from retouching a photo? (Answer: Retouching is done with the subject's knowledge and consent. The original negative remains. With the new technology there is no original and no basis upon which to judge truth or falsehood.)

3. Why do new ethical problems arise in society with the emergence of new technology?

4. If you cannot believe everything you read and you can't believe the pictures that go along with the news, what kinds of protective standards can be set to guarantee honest reporting of the facts? What is the basis for preferring one daily paper over another? (Sports section? Comics?) What do you think should be the basis for selecting a daily newspaper?

GA1328

A Picture Is Worth a Thousand Words

Improvisation—Role-Play Variations:

1. Role-play the scene at the photography seminar where a salesperson is demonstrating the new digital technology. This new age camera is based upon the capacity of the invention to alter a picture in ways which are not detectable. Some people in the audience are becoming aware that this state of the art equipment can be a threat to journalistic honesty. There is a great deal of audience participation and some concern from the potential customers.

2. Have a dialogue between two people. One person is trying desperately to explain to the other (a skeptic) just how the new technology can produce pictures that lie. It is especially difficult to impart the information that the hand-held digital cameras use a microchip instead of film. (If you were to return to the past, what other modern inventions would it be almost impossible for the ordinary person to describe to a citizen of the past? Try it.) (See "Big Dilemma: Trapped in the Past.")*

3. Improvise a meeting of several members of a tabloid staff. Your newspaper is called *The Daily Slander* and it sells in supermarkets and newsstands. The staff has put together some outrageous montage photos combining big celebrities in sports, entertainment, and politics who don't even know each other. With the new technology it was easy as pie. Describe the fabricated pictures your group has produced. What was the motivation? What consequences could result?

---

*Greta B. Lipson, Ed.D. *Fast Ideas for Busy Teachers* (Carthage, Illinois: Good Apple, Inc., 1989), p. 13.

GA1328

A Picture Is Worth a Thousand Words

Writing Suggestions:

1. If you could change the history of a particular event or era in history by manipulating the recorded pictures of that time, what event would it be? Explain your choice. How would that change be good or bad for humankind?

2. Have the teacher read the Associated Press article on page 75, "Photo helps to clear man; he heads back to school." Relative to this case, write a paragraph which explains the quote, "Justice delayed is justice denied." How would the new age cameras affect Malcolm Emory's capacity to prove he was wrongfully accused of assault on the campus of Northeastern University? (His picture was taken *before* such tampering was possible. Had the technology existed then, he would not have been able to prove anything.)

3. In ancient times when a courier brought bad news to the king which angered him, the king had the power to issue the command, "Kill the messenger!" Today we still use the term figuratively. A modern example of "Kill the messenger" was found recently in the "Letters to the Editor" of a big city newspaper. A coalition of civic, religious, and business leaders charged that the public was bombarded by headlines and photos which focused on a particular neighborhood. This suggested to the coalition that one segment of the population was always targeted, by the newspaper, as being responsible for crime and violence. For that reason, the civic-minded leaders were encouraging the readers to boycott the newspaper. Both sides agreed that the city did have serious problems. The newspaper people insisted, however, that the photographers and journalists simply reported those problems. The editor said, "The newspaper reflects the news—it does not create it! Boycotting newspapers will not make the city's social problems go away!" Who is right and why? Express your written opinion.

4. The word *context* means "that which surrounds something and influences its meaning." Context is important in photojournalism, in order to interpret what is seen. Pretend you are shown a picture of a man holding a club over another man's head. Write two opposite ways in which the picture could be interpreted if there were no context to depend upon?

GA1328

Chapter 7
A Picture Is Worth a Thousand Words
The Camera Catches a Moment of Truth
Student Comment

Characters: Grandma, Iris Leica
      Grandchild, Nelly Nikon
      Salesperson
      Camera customers

· ·

 In a paragraph express your feelings about any aspect of this story which you liked or disliked. How would you have changed it?

Alternative: Now that the story has been discussed, explain the proverb above from your point of view.

· ·

_____

_____

_____

_____

GA1328

Chapter 8
The Bully

GA1328

Chapter 8
The Bully
Synopsis

The scene is set at Anytown High School where Timmy Coy, a skinny little "brain," and big Bruce the Moose get into an altercation in the hall. Timmy gets a bloody nose and everyone is outraged with this act of aggression by Moose. Appearing quickly on the scene is diminutive custodian Ms. Milly, who has a reputation as the greatest mediator in the school. The crowd collects as a support group for the frail victim. Ms. Milly cuts to the heart of the matter with surprising insights about the role each disputant played as victim and aggressor. Through the unexpected ending, Milly acts as a rugged model for student conflict resolution in the future.

GA1328

Chapter 8
The Bully

Anatomy Is Destiny

By Greta B. Lipson

You know how they make jokes about who really runs Anytown High School? Well, if you could hear the stories about the custodian who cleans up when school closes, you'd understand. We all call her Ms. Milly, and there's nothing that goes on in those corridors or behind administrative doors that she doesn't know about. She's known far and wide as a fighter for truth and justice, protector of the underdog, and advocate for the rights of the little people.

Our favorite question to ask newcomers is "Have you met Ms. Milly yet? She's dynamite! About five feet tall (1.52 m), a keen eye, and quick as electric to analyze a tough situation. She's one of the most important people around here."

Or else we simply say, "What's the best-known secret at Anytown High School? It's Ms. Milly the Mediator who runs the school. She's the smartest peacemaker these kids have ever seen."

Sometimes Ms. Milly is slow and diplomatic, but sometimes she takes short-cuts and just jumps right into the argument. One of her greatest cases involved Bruce the Moose and Timmy Coy, that puny, sharp kid who belongs to all the brainy clubs. It all started outside of the gym. There were plenty of students milling around but nobody knew exactly what happened.

83

GA1328

Timmy was looking up at all six feet (1.82 m) of the Moose and was shouting like mad. You could tell that Timmy was just beginning to hit his stride and wasn't going to take it any more! Moose just stood there looking vacant with a half smile on his face that couldn't make up its mind. The two of them were standing toe to toe with Timmy making all the commotion. The veins were popping out of his scrawny little neck, and he was holding his ground in the face of brute strength.

There was lots of confusion and noise. Then before we knew it, Timmy came out of the ruckus with a bloody nose and his hand cupped under the dribbling mess. No question where the sympathy lay. A few good Samaritans handed him paper towelling to give his poor nose some help. Coach came running out of the gym just in time to miss everything and add to the upset. He started to herd us out of the corridor with the help of tough Ms. Trask, but feelings were running high so nobody was moving.

Nothing else serious happened, but Moose was standing there by the lockers and hadn't moved an inch since all the commotion started. Timmy's supporters were confronting the big guy because they felt safe in the crowd. "Who you gonna go after next—my little sister or some runt with glasses?"

They were outraged by this demonstration of raw power and were full of admiration for Timmy's self-defense attack on Moose. Coach was trying to sort through the charges and countercharges—but you didn't have to be a genius to see that the score was zero for Moose and 100 percent for

Timmy. Finally Ms. Milly showed up. The crowd reverently parted for her, just as our abused little hero had gotten his nose under control. Her very presence created a mood of respect and the kids quieted. Timmy was going to have his final hour of glory with Ms. Milly on the case. "Go get 'em, Ms. Milly. We hate bullies." Bruce the Moose was in for it now!

All eyes were on the diminutive custodian. "You got it right, kids. Everybody hates a bully no matter who it is—big or small, dumb or smart. And that means you—Timothy Coy."

Her remarks caused an uproar. "No, no. Wait a minute, Ms. Milly. Let Moose have it. You got it wrong. Go after Moose."

"I don't have anything wrong." Her eyes swept in the group. She talked right at Timmy and wagged her finger under his injured shnozolo. "You're the one who's been goading the Moose for weeks with insults about big guys with muscles and no brains—as if you were some kind of kindergartner. When you saw he didn't react, you kept pushing him further and further as if there were no limits to his temper. It upset you, didn't it, when you couldn't get a rise out of him? Be honest."

Someone whispered, "She must have eyes in the back of her head. I didn't know Timmy was such a nerd." The crowd was bewildered by this unexpected turn of events.

GA1328

Timmy tried to regain lost ground. "We were just having a little fun," he said, "shadow boxing and stuff like that, when Moose went too far." His story was too late and not very convincing.

Ms. Milly just kept chooching ahead. "It was you who went too far, Timmy. You found out that you could get away with anything because Moose would never hurt a soul. So you just kept on with your insults and your pestering till he'd had it with you."

"Yeh and that's when he bloodied my nose!" Timmy whined.

"That's not true," Moose finally opened his mouth for the first time. All eyes turned his way. "I kept telling him to shut up, but he wouldn't. It was downright embarrassing. Always poking me, daring me to show muscle and me all the time asking him to back off. The kid's a big pain in the neck."

A voice from the sidelines demanded, "So get to the nose part, already. It didn't just start bleeding by itself!" The Timmy partisans were not quite so sure about things, now.

"Yeh, that's right—how do you explain that, Moose?" a few other busybodies joined in.

It was an expectant moment. Bruce the Moose wasn't such a sweetheart anymore. He had taken all the abuse he could. "I'll tell you how I explain it. I just grabbed Timmy by the collar and lifted him off his feet to get him out of my face. He started flailing his arms around like a monkey on a stick, and before I knew it he bopped himself a good wallop right in his own nose."

Ms. Milly stepped into the forum once again. "You, Timmy boy, have a job to do on yourself, then—like it or not— you've got to get together with Moose for a talk. As for the rest of you, keep in mind what I said before— that bullies come in all sizes and they can be real dumb, real smart, or in between."

Everyone who had ever had a rotten experience with a troublemaker, big or small, got the message. The chastened crowd dispersed, as the little custodian chalked up another victory for the underdog.

GA1328

The Bully

Point of View—Discussion Questions:

1. The crowd in the hall at Anytown High School was quick to condemn Bruce the Moose as the villain in the bloody nose episode with little Timmy Coy. Why were they so quick to assume that Moose was guilty?

Possible Answer:

In the history of conflict where "might makes right," it is often true that the strong victimize the weak. In a conflict between big and small people, we automatically assume the big one to be the bully and the small one to be the victim. One of the problems in being a big strong person is that many people expect certain behaviors from larger people, even when they are children. Because of stereotyping, the expectation is that if you are big you are also physical, tough and ready for a fight. If you should defend yourself in a threatening situation you may likely be labelled a bully—even though you acted appropriately. Bullying is more complicated than the size of the bully.

2. In this story Ms. Milly, the custodian, helps resolve the conflict between Timmy and Moose—but there are methods by which students themselves can be their own mediators. Do you believe the following strategy for

88

GA1328

"conflict resolution" would work in your class or school with some practice: When a bad situation arises, the two "disputants" get together with fellow students who act as "problem busters." The first step requires that the two antagonists listen to each other's complaints, with the understanding that both of them must work toward solving the difficulty. Each person explains his/her grievances which contribute to the conflict. Each offers solutions for a compromise toward better relations. This is done with the supportive efforts of the helping students. There is no adult intervention. The adult role is involved only with training and practice for the conflict resolution strategy. If you believe this student-initiative could work (or would not work) in your class, explain your reasons why. What do you believe are the strengths and weaknesses of this approach?*

3. Webster's definition of a *sterotype* is ". . . a standardized mental picture that is held in common by members of a group and that represents an oversimplified opinion, affective attitude, or uncritical judgement." In this story Moose's large size is the problem and the reason he was assumed to be guilty. What other groups of people are victims of stereotyping and suffer the consequences where size is not the issue?

4. Size discrimination is a problem for large people. Conversely, small people also experience particular attitudes and are treated in ways they find to be offensive. Can you describe what these attitudes may be? What difficulties may small people have in their daily environment? How does the term *Little Caesar* or *Little Napoleon* support a steroetype?

---

*Jeanne Gordon, in Los Angeles, "Teaching Kids to Negotiate," *Newsweek*, April 23, 1990, p. 65.
See also: Carl Rogers's "Self-reflective" therapy.

GA1328

The Bully

Improvisation—Role-Play Variations:

1. Role-play the episode between Timmy Coy and Bruce the Moose, which led up to the action in the story—or play the scene as it occurred in the corridor of Anytown High School with the crowd on the spot.

2. Moose and Timmy (or any other disputants of choice) are in a private session where students are conducting the proceedings. The students want to resolve the conflict between Moose and Timmy and are acting as problem busters between these two hostile characters. Using the guidelines outlined in discussion question #2, role-play a conflict resolution strategy. The scenario is the choice of the role-play participants.

3. Five distinct student types participate in a mock school meeting and are standing in front of the class. Each participant gets a private "clue card" which explains the personality of the character role to be performed, as follows:

   - an optimist who thinks all ideas are wonderful
   - an enthusiastic leader with good ideas
   - a whiner who thinks everything was better at his other school
   - a painfully shy person who has no ideas
   - a person who is hostile to everyone

The mock meeting is called to order for the purpose of generating ideas that will express school spirit. The actors give strong clues that reveal their personality characteristics. In the discussion that follows the role play, what is the audience perception of each personality? What problems would present themselves in dealing with each of these people if they were obliged to get along with one another and produce results?

The Bully

Writing Suggestions:

1. Sometimes a self-fulfilling prophecy is at work and people act out a role—or become the kind of person that others expect them to be. This may be true of a bully, a smart mouth, a comic, a cool dude, or someone who is in outer space. Being what others expect you to be can be a terrible burden. Write about an incident you have observed where you thought such factors were at play. Have you ever been that person?

2. Entitle your paper "First Impression." Just as the crowd at Anytown High misjudged Bruce the Moose and Timmy Coy, many people misjudge others after having met them very briefly. You may perceive a person to be snobbish, gruff, cold, or foolish, and you could be terribly wrong. Recollect an incident when you made a snap judgment about someone and then discovered that your first impression was way off base.

3. Handicapped people (Handicappers) are another group of people who are often misunderstood and are stereotyped as being inadequate. At the University of Cambridge, England, there is a professor who is a paraplegic. He cannot walk, speak, or feed himself. He has Lou Gehrig's disease (amyotrophic lateral sclerosis), a progressive disease of the central nervous system, and is confined to a wheelchair. His name is Stephen M. Hawking (1942—) and despite his handicap, he is one of the world's greatest theoretical physicists. Make an effort to find a review of his life and his book, *A Brief History of Time: From the Big Bang to Black Holes.* Write a paragraph of your impressions of Hawking's achievements despite his devastating handicap. (Hawking typed the manuscript of his book one letter at a time, by using a stick in his mouth.)

GA1328

Chapter 8
The Bully
Anatomy Is Destiny
Student Comment

Characters: Ms. Milly, custodian   Ms. Trask, teacher
                Timmy Coy   Coach
                Bruce the Moose

. . . .

In a paragraph express your feelings about any aspect of this story which you liked or disliked. How would you have changed it?

Alternative: Now that the story has been discussed, explain the proverb above from your point of view.

. . . .

GA1328

Chapter 9
There's a Sucker Born Every Minute

GA1328

Chapter 9
There's a Sucker Born Every Minute
Synopsis

Phil Flam, a con artist, goes into business selling Phil Flam's Famous Elixir which cures coughs, colds, sore moles, pimples on the belly, and asthma! He sells his miracle medicine from the contrived stage of his motorized prairie schooner at state fairs and special events. He is a man with a "silver tongue" who easily commands great crowds and a loyal following. One day Phil falls from the platform in a siege of acute illness as his concerned customers rush to his rescue. He has unwittingly set the stage for his own ignominious end.*

---

*Based upon an Aesop Fable, "The Shoemaker Turned Doctor."

GA1328

Chapter 9
There's a Sucker Born Every Minute
The Gullible Support the Sharpers
By Greta B. Lipson

There was this guy, Phil Flam, who sold shoes over in the general store in Grand Bend. Nobody could figure out how he did it, but his sales were phenomenal. He knew just what to say to people to charm them half senseless. It was a kind of intuition he had that never failed him. He was like the grand master of "folksy psychology," and he never even took a course. Matter of fact this guy hardly went to school at all and had never graduated from grade 3.

His family had figured him for a bum who couldn't do much of anything. Seems like he never shut his mouth long enough to learn from his studies. His teacher had the same complaint. But everybody had to admit he talked really well—like a man with a silver tongue. Watching him operate at the shoe store was the best sport around. Flam had more moves than an octopus! When he saw a skinny self-conscious runt he'd say, "Hi there, Tiger. Still making hearts flutter among the pretty girls in town?" The runt would smile self-consciously and then seem to be just a little inflated by the joshing. (Flam was never a smart mouth. He was always believable.) But we all figured that Phil's snow jobs worked because people believe what they want to, even when it doesn't make a whole lot of sense.

GA1328

If he was trying to sell to a tough guy he'd say, "I can tell that nobody puts anything over on you, and I'm not the one to try, but confidentially I want you to know . . . ." And then he'd say something conspiratorial to the chump who'd fall for it every time. Or else he'd say—like he was dying to know, "Can I ask you a personal question? Are you a weight lifter?"

When a young woman would come in with a testy attitude, Phil would move in real easy and say something like, "I know how it feels, Missy, when people don't understand you, but that's the way it is when you're not like everybody else in the whole town. If it's shoes you're lookin' for, I have a pair that would fit your unique personality to a T. They have your special flair written all over them."

GA1328

Little by little the toughest cynics would fall for his line 'cause there are some things we are all just dying to believe—like when Phil Flam would look the ladies straight in the eye and tell them, "That's the most becoming hair-do ever. I'll bet you came right here straightaway from the beauty parlor." He always came up a winner.

Pretty soon Flam sensed that he was wasting his considerable talent selling shoes. It was abundantly clear that he could sell anybody anything. An idea for his own business struck him when he visited the state fair one lucky day and listened to the hawkers sell their wares. He'd watch them deliver a persuasive spiel as the crowds would begin to gather 'round and every person was hypnotized and just dying to buy something. He was inspired to become a medicine man with a motorized prairie schooner—which looked all the world like a covered wagon from the old West. He concocted a pale amber elixir, made from a good portion of simple syrup, a hint of alcohol, and a nice dose of sarsaparilla. Then he funneled the stuff into eight-ounce (236.59 ml) medicine bottles. The labels on the bottles had a picture of Phil looking as sincere as a body could look and still be human. Calling himself Doc Phil Flam, he hit all the small towns on the circuit and worked the crowds at all the fairs. Oh how the money rolled in!

The golden tones of his resonating voice mesmerized the customers as he chanted the wonders of Flam's health tonic. They loved and adored him as he peddled the powers of his brew:

> "Be a better husband,
> A more radiant wife
> You've never felt
> So good in your life."

Flam's tonic cures:
> "Coughs, colds,
> Sore moles,
> Pimples on the belly
> And asthma!"

The people believed every word as Phil's litany floated from the make-shift stage. The folks sang his praises and testified to the curative powers of Flam's bottled amber liquid, 'till one sorrowful day when Phil Flam fell ill right smack in front of his own audience. The ten-dollar bills from his sales were still bulging out of his vest and trouser pockets when he was stricken—toppling from the stage and clutching his belly in agony.

"Call a doctor, quick," he groaned.

"No need to call one of them quacks, Phil. Take a swig of your own Flam's Famous Elixir. That'll cure what ails you," his fans assured him.

"I don't want it," he croaked. "Don't you understand. Call a doctor now," Flam implored.

"Don't be a fool, Doc—you've been healing us all this time—now it's your turn to get healed."

"I feel like I'm going to die, for sure," he blubbered, holding his sides.

A sympathetic customer in the crowd actually gave up his own bottle of Phil Flam's Famous Elixir. Others held the Doc down and forcibly poured it into his throat. They soothed and reassured him that it would make him as good as new. He choked and fussed, battling them to no avail. By now he was crying like a babe, "You dumb louts! This stuff won't cure anything! It's about as good as a moonshiner's rot gut."

Everybody stopped—frozen into a tableau of stunned silence. In a hushed whisper a question filled the air, "Did you hear what he said?"

"Sure we heard him. He said he's been selling us worthless rot gut!"

99

GA1328

The crowd was angered and humiliated. Finally a vengeful voice shouted out, "Hang the rotten weasel!"

But cooler heads prevailed as another customer said, "Why make trouble for yourself over someone who ain't worth a sack of garbage?" They turned their backs on Phil Flam and left the charlatan to his own ignominious fate, groveling in the dirt.

GA1328

There's a Sucker Born Every Minute

For the Teacher:

2B Detroit Free Press/Friday, June 1, 1990*

Where are the prizes? 3 charged with scam

by Jocelyne Zablit
Free Press Staff Writer

Georgia Rogers said that when a St. Clair Shores firm told her she was the lucky winner of a 1990 Cadillac, she thought the deal was too good to be true—but also too good to pass up.

A company spokesman told her that for just $599, she could claim her prize, the 67-year-old Waco, Texas, retiree said Thursday.

"I thought it was surely real," Rogers said. "I heard of people winning like that in sweepstakes. But the more I thought about it after I mailed the check the more I became skeptical."

But by then it was too late.

On Thursday, IRS agents and St. Clair Shores police arrested three members of the firm—Greater Michigan Marketing—and charged them with fraud.

Owner Frank Pullano, 42, of St. Clair Shores, manager Merrit Bushman, 33, of Mt. Clemens and employee Ronald Prebee, 24, of Warren each face up to five years in prison and $250,000 in fines if convicted.

> "The more I thought about it after I mailed the check the more I became skeptical."
> **Georgia Rogers**

Their attorney, Brian Legghio, declined comment Thursday.

The trio and others allegedly called at least 129 people throughout the country with promises of a car, a trip to the Bahamas, a 48-inch television or cash. They were told the company distributes vitamins and they should send money for vitamins and for taxes on the prizes, federal officials said.

IRS spokeswoman Sarah Wreford said the firm, which has two offices in St. Clair Shores and one in East Detroit, took in at least $70,000.

Caroline Colvin, 79, of Bellflower, Calif., said she was told to send $399 to claim one of four prizes, but the firm settled on $200 since she couldn't afford the larger amount.

"I was foolish," she said Thursday. "I've never done anything like that. It was my mistake."

Rogers said she tries not to get worked up about the matter. "I am angry but I can't afford to have a heart condition and fall to pieces and get sick," she said. "I would have needed that much to go to the hospital."

---

*Reprinted with permission of Robert McGruder, Managing Editor/News. *The Detroit Free Press*, Detroit, Michigan.

There's a Sucker Born Every Minute

Point of View—Discussion Questions:

1. Why do people believe the promises, the sales pitch or the claims of persons like Phil Flam, who are con artists? What explains the gullibility of the public who fall for such chicanery?

Possible Answer:

P.T. Barnum, the showman of circus fame, was purported to have said, "There's a sucker born every minute." But long before that, the ancient Aesop in his famous fables told the story of a shoemaker turned doctor who victimized people and got into the same trouble as Phil Flam. Aesop's story reveals to us that there were gullible people even 2500 years ago.* Among the many reasons people are duped is that they want to believe what they hear; they may be searching for a miracle cure; they may be greedy and eager to make a fast dollar; or they want to improve their appearance. Perhaps there is an innocence in the basic nature of human beings that makes them wish that a remedy for problems is within reach. Perhaps, too, there is the eternal hope that it is possible to get something for almost nothing!

2. In your opinion, what type of person becomes a flimflam artist? If there is talent involved, what kinds of skills does such a person have that makes others trust him or her?

3. Why is it unreasonable when advertisements promise a "get rich quick" offer or want to give you something for nothing? What offers do you know about which should make people suspicious and are found daily on TV, radio, or in the print media? Collect some questionable advertisements that sound too good to be true. Bring them to class for analysis. (Remember the warning of the Better Business Bureau which states, "If it sounds too good to be true, it probably is.")

---

*For other cautionary tales to live by, see *Famous Fables for Little Troupers*, by Greta B. Lipson, Ed.D. (Carthage, Illinois: Good Apple, Inc., 1984).

GA1328

There's a Sucker Born Every Minute

Improvisation—Role-Play Variations:

1. Role-play a scene at the state fair where Phil Flam is making a sales pitch for his elixir to a captive audience. They obviously love him and his cure-all medicine.

2. Invite customers onto the makeshift stage in front of the motorized covered wagon. These eager people will give testimonials on how Phil Flam's Famous Elixir cured them of some disabling illnesses and restored them to health and vigor. They claim their lives were mercifully changed for the better.

3. Enact the last scene where Phil Flam is deathly sick and members of his well-intentioned audience are trying to force him to drink his own phoney elixir. As the scene ends, there are varying reactions to the revealed truth that Flam is a phoney. Anger moves people in different ways. Some want to go after Phil's hide right there on the spot. A few quieter citizens consider a legal solution to make him pay for his villainy! And then there are those folks who are very embarrassed over their own stupidity.

4. In a group effort, present a "hard-sell" commercial to the class. Select a product or a service among the many you have seen, such as a weight loss program, a dating service, an exterminator, or a teacher machine for correcting papers. Use props and visual aids. Select the group that had the most outrageous sales pitch.

There's a Sucker Born Every Minute

Writing Suggestions:

1. Acting as a consumer affairs group, write an after-school special on con artists, swindlers, and imposters. Warn consumers about how to avoid being exploited by fraudulent or questionable advertisers. Give advice to unsuspecting citizens by describing ploys that are used to prey on the public. Contact your local consumer affairs government agency for additional information.

2. Write a misleading TV, radio, or newspaper advertisement for any product or service. Include claims that have no substance in fact. Try to be convincing when presenting these "come-on" lures to the class: "Lose weight and eat as much as you want." "Grow rich thick hair in a few weeks!" "Be a top executive in thirty days with our dynamic instruction." "Develop into a powerful persuasive speaker after twelve mail order lessons." "Want to knock the girls (or guys) dead with your charm . . .?" "Earn money like a Wall Street wizard and triple your life savings!"

3. Review advertisements in the print media which make liberal use of propaganda techniques. Copy the exact words and phrases. Try to identify the techniques on the next page.

Glittering Generalities:
  Shimmer shampoo makes your hair bouncier and alluring.

Plain Folks:
  Wheat bread like Grandma used to make

Emotional Appeal:
  If your love is forever, give her (him) . . . .

Testimonial:
  The great Butch Kurlansky buys Bruiser Sweat Socks.

Scientific Approach:
  Four out of five board certified dentists use Dazzler toothpaste.

Snob Appeal:
  For those in prestigious positions who want to drive in elegance . . .

Bandwagon:
  Join the savvy, hip kids in your generation and wear cuneiforms.

Transfer:
  (Grouping unrelated things for a stronger effect):
    Young and carefree (Is that always true?)

    Thick and juicy (Can't it be thick and tough?)

    Homegrown and delicious (Can it be homegrown and inferior?)

GA1328

Chapter 9
There's a Sucker Born Every Minute
The Gullible Support the Sharpers
Student Comment

Characters: Phil Flam, the flimflam man
             Customers at the state fair

· ·

In a paragraph express your feelings about any aspect of this story which you liked or disliked. How would you have changed it?

Alternative: Now that the story has been discussed, explain the proverb above from your point of view.

· ·

_____

_____

_____

_____

_____

Chapter 10
The Destiny of David Swan

Chapter 10
The Destiny of David Swan
Synopsis

David Swan is a young man who leaves the farm and is on his way to Boston where an uncle has offered him a job in the grocery trade. He walks to the nearest town in the summer heat to wait for the Boston coach. Once there he finds a secluded, mystical little park in which to rest his weary self. Almost as soon as David rolls up his knapsack and puts it under his head, he falls into a deep, delicious slumber. While he sleeps, other characters enter his life fleetingly. Fate stands by teasing his future. A chance at wealth and privilege presents itself, a blissful romance with a lovely woman becomes a possibility, and even Death, a sinister and unexpected guest, waits for David. Through all of these possibilities, the young man sleeps unaware—and finally awakens as he must—to his actual fate.

Chapter 10
The Destiny of David Swan*

Fate Is a Dark Secret Concealed from Us All

Retold by Greta B. Lipson

It was harder to say good-bye this morning than he had ever dreamed it could be. But David Swan told himself that he was no longer a child—it was time to leave and make a life for himself elsewhere. There was no future on the farm, he knew it well, but still he was wrenched by the decision and was even a little fearful.

They had all walked out of the house with him—his mother and father, sister and brothers, and of course the dog who faced his loss stoically. And when David turned away to leave, he felt the emotional presence of his family at his back. They were standing—framed by the old house—watching him. He thought that if he allowed himself to look at them one last time their arms would be outstretched as if to call him back in silent remorse at his departure.

---

*Retold from "David Swan," *The Complete Short Stories of Nathaniel Hawthorne: Seventy-Two Tales of Fantasy and Imagination* (Garden City, New York: Doubleday and Company, Inc., 1959).

GA1328

The offer of a job from his uncle in Boston came at just the right time. David would be a clerk in the grocery trade, and if he did well and worked hard there would be no telling about the promise of the future. His heart lightened somewhat out of gratitude toward a relative he had never met.

He had set out from the farm at sunrise and was now walking under the blazing noon sun of an August day. The coach wasn't due for at least an hour when he arrived at the center of town. That would be just enough time for David to rest his feet and get relief from the sweltering heat. Surprised and grateful, he found a little grove of trees nestled on a patch of green just off the main street. The leaves arched above like a cool, lacy umbrella as he eased himself onto the soft grass and contemplated the fountain with its offerings of refreshment. No one could have imagined such a secluded retreat in the heart of this bustling intersection.

GA1328

The bundle of clothes he carried made a soft cushion roll for his head. He stretched out with the intention of enjoying the blue sky filtering through the graceful branches. The cool earth yielded under him. As could be expected he was lulled by the calm of the scene and was swept into a deliciously deep sleep.

Some passersby noticed the young man sleeping soundly. One righteous fellow thought David was in a drunken stupor and included this anecdote in a temperance speech he was to be giving that evening on the evils of drink. Another person saw David and reflected on the pure innocence of his face. Life went on and the farm boy was left alone in his slumber.

Within moments after he had fallen asleep, a fine carriage pulled up at the miniature park and an older, obviously affluent couple stepped out of the carriage. A wheel needed fixing and their servant was preparing to help the coachman with the repairs. The elderly merchant and his wife were returning to Boston and were pleased with this green enclave which offered its gentle shade. Immediately they noticed David and remarked upon the good fortune of the young who could enjoy such relaxed and untroubled sleep—for the weary merchant had the serious problems which beset the very rich.

GA1328

The merchant and his wife carried with them a burden of grief, for they had lost a son, who was their only heir, and there was no one left to whom they could leave their considerable fortune. The wife looked at the slumbering David and perceived a resemblance to their unfortunate, dead son, Henry. She was overcome with emotion, as only a parent could be who had lost a child. She suggested to her husband that they should waken the young lad to discover his true goodness. For he had the appearance of a worthy young man. Perhaps a generous stroke of luck had brought them all together so that this boy could take the place of their own departed Henry.

At that critical moment with ". . . fortune bending over David just ready to let fall a burden of gold," the servant announced that their coach was repaired and ready to travel once again. The old couple were jolted back to reality. They left the park feeling foolish about their effusive impulse toward a young man who was, to them, a total stranger.

No sooner had they departed than a pretty girl walked briskly over the grassy berm into the privacy of the trees. Emily was her name, and she was having a struggle with a broken garter and a falling stocking that had to be rescued out of public view. The park afforded her just the seclusion she needed.

She almost fell over the slumbering David and was so shocked that she blushed, though no one had seen the closeness of the mishap. Emily was overcome with his handsome appearance. "So like a prince," she thought. "He could be my life's companion, and we would make a perfect, loving twosome." She knew he was the right romantic partner for her. It was a strong intuitive sense that filled her with yearning. If only he would open his eyes and instantly discover the same feelings for her.

Emily's father had announced that she was of an age to be married. He was already searching for another person to work in his business, for he was a thriving country merchant. Such a man as David would be considered a candidate for a son-in-law as well. Her father was, as usual, forthcoming about his plans for her. Perhaps it was because she was never consulted in important matters related to her life, that at this very moment, looking at David, she wished desperately that her father's choice could be this noble looking youth whose name was unknown to her.

Though such a radiant future was so close to realization for David, he slept and remained blissfully unconscious of it. What a pity. In a parting gesture Emily brushed her handkerchief against a bee about to settle on David's eyelid, but still he slept without stirring. The shy girl left, bearing her disappointment, as she looked longingly at David one more time.

Sweet Emily walked out of David's life forever, when two suspicious looking men entered the park. They were furtive, dressed in rough attire, with caps pulled down over their eyes looking as if they were about some kind of mischief. And indeed they were. Any chance to turn a dollar would satisfy them, no matter how low the enterprise. They spied David almost immediately and were overjoyed that they had stumbled onto a likely, unconscious victim. No doubt about it, they thought. This was a country bumpkin who probably had an ample roll of cash in the bundle tucked under his head.

Almost with one mind they talked over the quick plan. One of them would search the bundle and the other, who brandished a knife, would hold it to David's heart. If the boy were to awaken while they were about their dirty business, he would be stabbed through the heart swiftly and perhaps they would be richer for the whole incident. They undertook the task with great relish and not a moment's hesitation since they had neither scruples nor decency to deter them. David made things so much easier since he slept like a stone.

114

GA1328

All at once there was a tromping sound crashing through the underbrush as a hound of terrifying proportions came shambling out of the green hedges. The lumbering beast sniffed his way into the park, curiously. He eyed the bandits cautiously and then looked at the inert form lying on the ground. This was not a dog to be trifled with. The threat of the animal was an unwelcome turn of events for the two thieves. There was not a moment of indecision when the rascals decided that such a well-groomed monster must have a powerful master who would appear very soon to threaten their thievery. They took off as fast as they could and cursed their rotten luck besides.

All of this had taken place in one single hour. David stirred slowly from his restful sleep to a moderately conscious state—just in time to hear the stagecoach arrive in a clatter of sounds and noises from the passengers. He roused himself hurriedly, brushed his clothes and appeared on the street shouting to the driver. "Hey there. Wait up for another passenger!" He waved furiously to catch the driver's attention.

115

GA1328

"You're lucky," the driver shouted back, "We have room for one more, and that's it."

As David settled in for the final part of his trip to Boston, he reflected on his quiet life on the farm, wondering in silent yearning if anything truly eventful awaited him. Probably not. His would be a commonplace, humdrum world moving on into the contentent of maturity. Excitement would elude him. Fate would not extend to him the heady chance at power or wealth, nor the sweet gift of sublime romantic love. Least of all—he would never, ever experience a brush with life-threatening adventure to quicken the pulse.

"Oh, well. What's the use?" he sighed. "Nothing exciting ever happens to me."

GA1328

The Destiny of David Swan

Point of View—Discussion Questions:

1. If it is true that our lives are determined by the whims of fate, or destiny or chance, how do we have any influence over the course of events in our lives?

   Possible Answer:
   It would be foolish to deny the role of fate in the scenario of our lives or to deny the inexorable forces of nature or the unremitting effect of social class on all of us. There is so much that is in place for each of us at the time of birth that, some argue, we are almost programmed for our destiny. Others believe that we are the masters of our destiny. Included in this calculation, of course, is the effect of the country in which we live—and our relative freedom, health, education, or personal drive. Even our birth order makes a difference in our lives—if one is the oldest, middle, or youngest in the family. But all things considered—we definitely do make decisions every day of our lives. We do make important choices which have a profound effect upon the quality of our present and our future. To this degree we have some influence upon events and factors which shape our destiny.

2. Consider the decisions that you have the freedom to make on a daily basis. What choices do you make that could have a significant long-term effect on your future? How could a bad decision with regard to the friends you choose be of major importance? Think in terms of school, friends, recreation, and work. Be specific about positive and negative outcomes with regard to your choices.

3. There seems to be some people to whom bad things always happen. A philsopher said, in considering this situation, "Experience without understanding or insight just turns out to be one rotten thing after another." What does that mean to you? Enlarge upon that message. How does your ability to assess information, ask questions, make decisions, and set standards for ethical behavior help you control your life?

4. The great English scientist, Sir Isaac Newton, in his third law of motion states that "For each action there is an equal and opposite reaction." Explain how you think that works in human relations.

GA1328

The Destiny of David Swan

Improvisation—Role-Play Variations:

1. Assume the role of a research person. Interview a class member who is enacting the part of a teacher, counselor, custodian, or any other interesting adult in the community. Find out what brought them to their career choices and what elements of decision making or fate were factored into their careers.

2. Role-play a scenario in which David awakens while either the old couple, Emily, or the thieves were present. Go beyond the moment in the park and play out the possibilities according to the vision of all the other actors involved in the chance encounter. What happens?

3. Interview David Swan in his home or place of business ten years from the date of his trip to Boston. Ask questions which will reveal to the audience precisely what has taken place in the life of this man who left home to become a clerk in his uncle's business. Does he have any words of advice? Make his life as fascinating, mysterious, or as dull as you wish. In how many directions can a life unfold?

The Destiny of David Swan

Writing Suggestions:

1. Taking a thread from the theme of David Swan, weave a story of your own fate if you were born of other parents in a different family or if you lived in Asia, Africa, the Middle East, England, or Eastern Europe. Write a description of this *"other"* you. How would your life be different? Use your imagination but retain realism. (You could be a beggar on the streets of a Third World nation at the age of four!)

2. Brainstorm a list of famous people. Write a serious or funny biographical sketch where fate intercedes and the life of a famous person takes another direction. What alternative circumstances took them into a different profession or route? (Example: Albert Einstein, one of the greatest scientists of all time: Assume that he did not take a job as a civil servant in a Swiss patent office. Instead—his friendly neighbors, who knew he played the fiddle, offered him a gig in a busy cafe. He accepted the job because he was very poor and needed the extra bucks. The job was so pleasant and satisfying that he didn't finish his doctoral dissertation nor did he pursue any of his research again! What would have happened to $E = MC_2$ and to the world of science?)

3. In Greek mythology the ancients believed that the pattern of a human's life was determined by the Fates, who were the three daughters of Zeus. The sisters were called collectively, the MOIRAI (MOY rye). Each had a special task—Clotho spun the thread of life with light and dark lines which represented sorrow and happiness. Lachesis twisted the thread which made a life strong or weak. And Atropos—the most frightening sister of all—cut the thread which determined the length of a life. The sisters knew the past and everything in the future and no force in the universe could change the course of human events as they designed it.*

Write a letter on your own behalf to Clotho, Lachesis, or Atropos and make a personal request. Good luck!

---

*Greta B. Lipson, Ed.D., and Sidney M. Bolkosky, Ph.D., *Mighty Myth: A Modern Interpretation of Greek Myths for the Classroom* (Carthage, Illinois: Good Apple, Inc., 1982).

GA1328

Chapter 10
The Destiny of David Swan
Fate Is a Dark Secret Concealed from Us All
Student Comment

Characters: David Swan
             Old couple
             Emily
             Robbers

. . . .

In a paragraph express your feelings about any aspect of this story which you liked or disliked. How would you have changed it?

Alternative: Now that the story has been discussed, explain the proverb above from your point of view.

. . . .

_____

_____

_____

_____

_____

_____

_____

_____

_____

_____

_____

_____

_____

_____

_____

_____

GA1328

Chapter 11
The Cremation of Sam McGee

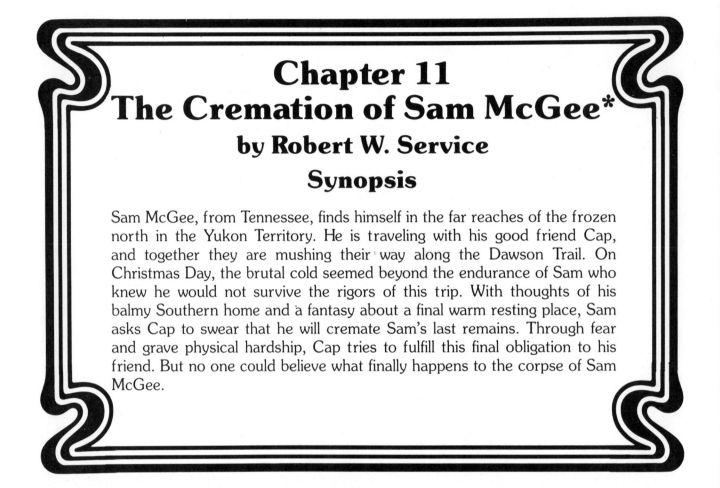

Chapter 11
The Cremation of Sam McGee*
by Robert W. Service
Synopsis

Sam McGee, from Tennessee, finds himself in the far reaches of the frozen north in the Yukon Territory. He is traveling with his good friend Cap, and together they are mushing their way along the Dawson Trail. On Christmas Day, the brutal cold seemed beyond the endurance of Sam who knew he would not survive the rigors of this trip. With thoughts of his balmy Southern home and a fantasy about a final warm resting place, Sam asks Cap to swear that he will cremate Sam's last remains. Through fear and grave physical hardship, Cap tries to fulfill this final obligation to his friend. But no one could believe what finally happens to the corpse of Sam McGee.

*Robert W. Service. "The Cremation of Sam McGee." Copyright 1907 by the Estate of Robert Service.

GA1328

Chapter 11
The Cremation of Sam McGee
by Robert W. Service
Courage Rises in the Face of Adversity

There are strange things done in the midnight sun
   By the men who toil for gold;
The Arctic trails have their secret tales
   That would make your blood run cold;
The Northern Lights have seen queer sights,
   But the queerest they ever did see
Was that night on the marge of Lake Lebarge
   I cremated Sam McGee.

Now Sam McGee was from Tennessee, where the cotton blooms
   and blows.
Why he left his home in the South to roam 'round the Pole,
   God only knows.
He was always cold, but the land of gold seemed to hold him like
   a spell;
Though he'd often say in his homely way that "he'd sooner live
   in hell."

GA1328

On a Christmas Day we were mushing our way over the
    Dawson Trail.
Talk of your cold! Through the parka's fold it stabbed like a
    driven nail.
If our eyes we'd close, then the lashes froze till sometimes we
    couldn't see;
It wasn't much fun, but the only one to whimper was Sam McGee.

And that very night, as we lay packed tight in our robes
    beneath the snow,
And the dogs were fed, and the stars o'erhead were dancing
    heel and toe,
He turned to me, and "Cap," says he, "I'll cash in this trip,
    I guess;
And if I do, I'm asking you that you won't refuse my last request."

Well, he seemed so low that I couldn't say no; then he says with
   a sort of a moan:
"It's the cursed cold, and it's got right hold till I'm chilled clean
   through to the bone.
Yet 'tain't being dead—it's my awful dread of the icy grave
   that pains;
So I want you to swear that, foul or fair, you'll cremate my last
   remains."

A pal's last need is a thing to heed, so I swore I would not fail;
And we started on at the streak of dawn but God! he looked
   ghastly pale.
He crouched on the sleigh, and he raved all day of his home
   in Tennessee;
And before nightfall a corpse was all that was left of Sam McGee.

125

GA1328

There wasn't a breath in that land of death, and I hurried, horror-driven,
With a corpse half hid that I couldn't get rid, because of a
    promise given;
It was lashed to the sleigh, and it seemed to say: "You may tax
    your brawn and brains,
But you promised true, and its up to you to cremate those last
    remains."

Now a promise made is a debt unpaid, and the trail has its own
    stern code.
In the days to come, though my lips were dumb, in my heart
    how I curse that load.
In the long, long night, by the lone firelight, while the huskies,
    round in a ring,
Howled out their woes to the homeless snows—O God! how
    I loathed the thing.

And every day that quiet clay seemed to heavy and heavier
grow;
And on I went, though the dogs were spent and the grub was
getting low;
The trail was bad, and I felt half mad, but I swore I would not
give in;
And I'd often sing to the hateful thing, and it hearkened with
a grin.

Till I came to the marge of Lake Lebarge, and a derelict there
lay;
It was jammed in the ice, but I saw in a trice it was called the
"Alice May."
And I looked at it, and I thought a bit, and I looked at my frozen
chum;
Then "Here," said I, with a sudden cry, "is my cre-ma-tor-eum."

Some planks I tore from the cabin floor, and I lit the boiler
   fire;
Some coal I found that was lying around, and I heaped the fuel
   higher;
The flames just soared, and the furnace roared—such a blaze you
   seldom see;
And I burrowed a hole in the glowing coal, and I stuffed in
   Sam McGee.

Then I made a hike, for I didn't like to hear him sizzle so;
And the heavens scowled, and the huskies howled, and the wind
   began to blow.
It was icy cold, but the hot sweat rolled down my cheeks, and I
   don't know why;
And the greasy smoke in an inky cloak went streaking down
   the sky.

GA1328

I do not know how long in the snow I wrestled with grisly fear;
But the stars came out and they danced about again I
    ventured near;
I was sick with dread, but I bravely said: "I'll just take a peep
    inside.
I guess he's cooked, and it's time I looked"; . . . then the door
    I opened wide.

And there sat Sam, looking cool and calm, in the heart of the
    furnace roar;
And he wore a smile you could see a mile, and he said: "Please
    close that door.
It's fine in here but I greatly fear you'll let in the cold and
    storm—
Since I left Plumtree, down in Tennessee, it's the first time I've
    been warm."

GA1328

There are strange things done in the midnight sun
    By the men who toil for gold;
The Arctic trails have their secret tales
    That would make your blood run cold;
The Northern Lights have seen queer sights,
    But the queerest they ever did see
Was that night on the marge of Lake Lebarge
    I cremated Sam McGee.

GA1328

The Cremation of Sam McGee

Point of View—Discussion Questions:

1. Define a hero. Establish criteria for any person, man or woman, whom you would consider to be a heroic character.

Possible Answer:

In an extraordinary article entitled "Do Teens Hunger for Heroes?" in *Seventeen* magazine, July 1981, the author, Ron Powers, establishes the following standards for a true hero: • "A hero must take risks • A hero must take the risk voluntarily • His or her actions must benefit the world at large • Heroes redeem us"

(Redemption is changing one's behavior in response to a positive ideal.)

2. *Cap* was the name of Sam McGee's friend who, despite his desperate fear, kept his word to Sam. He cremated Sam on the *Alice May*, a derelict barge which was tied up on Lake Lebarge. According to the standards for a hero (which you have established), do you believe that Cap was courageous or heroic? Was he simply driven by fear, a motivation which is less noble? Does he fit the criteria for a hero? Why or why not?

3. We have called many people in popular culture heroes. But now, having defined a hero in more limited terms than in ordinary usage, our standards may have changed. Why does a sports figure, a person in entertainment, a politician, or a prisoner of war *not* qualify as a hero? Keep referring back to Ron Powers' definition as the acid test.

4. Does an act of courage or heroism always imply a physical act? Explain intellectual acts of courage. (Standing up publicly for an ideal or something you believe in, expressing an unpopular opinion, telling the truth—though you may be punished for it—or acts of civil disobedience may all be intellectual acts of courage.)

GA1328

The Cremation of Sam McGee

Improvisation—Role-Play Variations:

1. Weary and exhausted after his strange trip home, Cap shares the details of his adventures on the Dawson Trail with his comrades. They ask some very specific questions because they don't believe he was capable of such perseverance in the face of such odds. They especially don't believe the fantasy that Sam McGee expressed his gratitude to Cap from the heart of the fiery crematorium on the barge. Cap responds to the direct questions of his friends and tries vigorously to defend his reputation. Re-create this scene.

2. Cap returns to camp under a cloud. By his own admission he left the body of Sam McGee in the deep snow where there was not even the need to dig a grave. He is criticized harshly by his comrades for not bringing the body back. His defense is that it was senseless to risk his own life just to bring back a dead body. He thinks that such an attitude is illogical. He believes that dragging the body back would have been a meaningless ritual. Some of his friends agree with his logic, others disagree. Assume a point of view for the role play. Generalize two other situations. For example, should a soldier on a field of battle risk his life to rescue the body of a dead comrade in arms? A boy or a girl can assume the role of Cap.

3. Assume the role of a real male or female hero in history. Be prepared to answer questions from the audience about your selfless act. Since self-preservation is the ultimate law of existence, how can it be that you were prepared to sacrifice yourself for the betterment of humankind?

(Prometheus in Greek mythology would be such a hero. He stole fire from the gods to give to humans. He wanted to elevate them from the level of animals and in doing so improve the quality of their lives. The name *Prometheus* means "forethought," which indicates that he knew fully that he would be punished eternally by the great god Zeus for having committed this act, but this did not deter him.)*

---

*Greta B. Lipson, Ed.D., and Sidney M. Bolkosky, Ph.D., *Mighty Myth: A Modern Interpretation of Greek Myths for the Classroom* (Carthage, Illinois: Good Apple, Inc., 1982).

GA1328

The Cremation of Sam McGee

Writing Suggestions:

1. In the poem, Cap expresses his reactions throughout his ordeal as follows: "It was icy cold but the hot sweat rolled down my cheeks," "I wrestled with grisly fear," "I was sick with dread." From your own experience or what you have heard, what do you think happens to a person physically in an emergency situation which makes it possible for that person to perform with power and speed? Write a description of your own personal reactions in a stressful situation which you have experienced. How does fright sometimes have a reverse reaction which does not produce courage or galvanize action?

2. Recall a heroic act which you have heard or read about currently or in history. Describe the circumstances. From the accounts of the situation, were there any clues about the reasons the hero would risk life and limb to help someone in trouble who may even have been a stranger? Do you believe such courage can be explained logically? Consider intellectual acts of courage as well.

3. Since "The Cremation of Sam McGee" was set in the frozen north, it would be intriguing to research the adventuresome Susan H. Butcher, dog kennel owner and famous "musher" who was, by 1990, a three-time winner of the Iditarod Trail Sled Dog Race in Alaska. The route of the race is from Anchorage to Nome—a formidable, tough 1600 miles of bitter, bone-chilling cold. If you could interview Ms. Butcher, what questions would you be anxious to ask this powerful woman who has met this Herculean challenge? For starters, you may want to know that she was born in Boston, Massachusetts, on December 26, 1954.

GA1328

Chapter 11
The Cremation of Sam McGee
Courage Rises in the Face of Adversity
Student Comment

Characters: Sam McGee from Tennessee
Cap, his friend
The men at camp

. . . .

In a paragraph express your feelings about any aspect of this story which you liked or disliked. How would you have changed it?

Alternative: Now that the story has been discussed, explain the proverb above from your point of view.

. . . .

_____

_____

_____

_____

_____

_____

_____

_____

_____

_____

_____

_____

_____

_____

_____

_____

_____

_____

Chapter 12
A Tail with a Twist

GA1328

Chapter 12
A Tail with a Twist
Synopsis

Mr. MacDonald, a contentious pig farmer, has lived on his Iowa farm, Oinker Acres, for as long as anybody can remember. Mr. Bud Pozey, a porcine land developer, buys the land next door to the farmer and builds Fragrant Meadows, a residential subdivision. In short time the residents realize that the farm is a serious nuisance, and they want to get rid of the inflexible Mr. MacDonald. But Old Mac refuses to leave his land. The residents are angry, and they take their grievance to the Francis Bacon Community Hall for a civic hearing. They claim that Old MacDonald stands in the way of progress. The outcome is unexpected! (Besides serving the cause of justice—this story has another twist: As you read it through, be a puckish punster and pick out pork parts and piggy allusions amply placed throughout this pugnacious tale. What's your score?)

GA1328

Chapter 12
A Tail with a Twist

Contentious People May Be Pigheaded

By Greta B. Lipson

Mr. MacDonald had owned the farm since he was a young guy. He settled far away from the city and through his desperately hard work Oinker Acres became the most prosperous pig farm in Iowa. As we all know—life changes and many years later the city grew toward the farm. That's when property developers bought the farm next door to Mac. They built houses in the meadow, put the babbling brook into a sewer, and then named the subdivision Fragrant Meadows.

Now something you have to know about Mac was that he had been a mean-spirited old coot even when he was young! Nobody ever got too familiar with him. Even his friends called him Mister. As his wife, Trichina, pointed out, he wasn't much for social amenities, but you couldn't make a silk purse out of a sow's ear. Besides, she said affectionately, he had other good qualities.

GA1328

On any morning, at Shoat's Cafe, over sausage and eggs, you could hear the ex-farmers gossiping about Old MacDonald and his pigheaded resistance to prosperity in the community. His former neighbors had all given up their farms, sold out to the developers, and joined the so-called wave of progress. But not Mac.

After the first families moved into Fragrant Meadows, things settled down for a while. Life was as smooth as a piglet's snout until the developers went hog-wild again. Bud Pozey, the builder, tried his level best to persuade Mac to sell his land. The "big boys" wanted that farm in the worst way. It seems the families in the subdivision were complaining that Old MacDonald was an intolerable nuisance.

138

GA1328

When the developers offered to cut a deal with Mac, he said to Trichina, "No sir! I'm not selling to those spoilers. Not in a pig's eye!" He was a stubborn rascal. Trichina and Mac knew they were lucky to get such fat offers for the farm. Besides that—Bud Pozey had even offered Mac a cushy-sounding job. But the old farmer didn't trust any of them. "Sounds like a pig in a poke to me!" he said. "Those guys are as slippery as a spoon in a lard bucket."

139

GA1328

The fact is that Mac loved his life as a farmer and though it demanded sacrifice and hardship, he cared deeply about the land. Both he and his wife had come from farming families, and it was all they had ever known. Besides that (and this may sound funny to you) Mac had an enduring affection for the porkers he raised. Trichina and Mac were determined to stay.

Maybe matters were resolved on the pig farm but the misery of the hapless residents at Fragrant Meadows increased daily. "No friendly barbecue parties for us anymore," Mr. Fretful announced. "That last experience was the pits, with all those barnyard smells floating in a cloud over the food on the picnic table. What a way to gag our dinner guests." To make matters worse, their kid, little Franny Fretful had a stuffed nose that was running nonstop from the pesticides in the air.

140

In another household Mrs. Barrow complained to her husband over the breakfast table. "How could that porcine builder, Bud Pozey, do this to us? What about zoning laws?" She had been listening to the roaring of MacDonald's tractor since sunrise.

Her husband was exasperated. "It's like I told you before—we're all properly zoned—Old MacDonald is zoned for his farm and we're zoned for our subdivision. Don't you get it? We're all legal, but the trouble is we're living side-by-side. Old Mac's not going to give up his farm, and we can't sell our house to anybody."

"It's time for a showdown," the residents decided. "We can't live next door to the stink, the chemicals, and the disgusting animal sounds, but Mac insists upon his property rights, too."

GA1328

Inevitably the neighbors took their grievance to the Francis Bacon Community Hall for a civic hearing. The place was jammed with people. Inside they were talking their heads off and outside it was crowded with protesters carrying placards. Some of the signs read: "Farmers have rights too."—"Oinker Acres is a public nuisance."—"Some slops don't care how they live."—"A pigsty is an eyesore."

After a long, heated meeting, the decision was announced by Hamilton Hocks who, though he was known to be a deadly bore, was always respected for his integrity. In a majority resolution, it was concluded that Old MacDonald's farm could stay just where it was and that was the final word.

GA1328

Before the meeting was dismissed, some angry folks stood up and shouted, "I don't believe this!"—"You call this justice? I call it hogwash!" "We demand an explanation!"

Old Hamilton Hocks rose from his seat and cleared his throat. There was a hush. "Old Mac has been on that farm for twenty-five years. Sure it's hog heaven and you don't like it. But remember. You folks made a choice and moved next door to a working farm of your own free will. Mac didn't move next door to you!"

The case is now in litigation in the courts in Suidae, Iowa. The complainants were not going to be hog-tied by a decison made at a civic hearing. This is a true story. Only the names have been changed to protect the innocent.

For the Teacher:

In the writing of educational books, it has been the author's practice to enlist the expertise of skillful people and, most especially, interested teachers who are willing to critique the material. The most fascinating result of all of this is discovering what others see in the material and how they would use it. Even more interesting, is the strong response a topic evokes! These responses are always a wonderful revelation to the author. The following incisive critique and social commentary, by Lorene Sterner, demonstrates this point, relative to "A Tail with a Twist." Her letter makes a strong case for teachers to use materials from whichever perspective they consider to be most effective!

May 31, 1990

Dear Greta,

I read the story and my opinion is that it is a good story. Good meaty issues (hardy har har). As someone who feels strongly about farms-turning-agribusiness, I would really love to see this story included, if only to get a little consciousness-raising out and about as to what is behind that styro-tray of pork chops you get in the supermarket.

The problem? You have embellished to the point where the story becomes a vocabulary-building exercise. It's amusing, but loses its "twist." I get no sense that MacDonald is, in fact, a character from real life (affection for pigs notwithstanding). I think you could make the point that many farmers have grown up on farms, know of no other life-style, and have worked extraordinarily hard to maintain their farms—gigantic loans, piles of paperwork to comply with federal rules for subsidies, plus the simple fact that farming is extremely dangerous. (I could tell you terrible stories of farm accidents that maim and kill but Bill could, too.) After a lifetime of devoting efforts to producing cheap, healthy food for the public, there should be some irony in being reviled as a public nuisance. As the bumper sticker says, "Farming is everybody's bread and butter."

And there is the fact that the need for affordable housing is tremendous. It's not luxury condos that are being built in these areas; rich people go where there are scenic views, room for their stables and tennis courts, and privacy. Farmlands tend to be developed into moderately priced (ha!) lots for families anxious to flee the crime and deterioration of the city. These are not people who can afford to litigate endlessly to stop what they perceive is a nuisance and a danger; we're talking a scenario more like Love Canal. There is more to the juxtaposition of farm and residential, though, than noise and offensive smells when the wind is right.

You can bet in a real-life situation there would be lawsuits against MacDonald for farm-related respiratory disorders (my father gets instantaneous pneumonia whenever he enters a hog barn); organic waste contaminating groundwater; pesticide/herbicide spray drifting into the subdivision and leading to more respiratory problems, central nervous system disorders and cancer. There would probably be a left-wing protest against inhumane penning and treatment of food animals, too, with charges that MacDonald uses antibiotics and hormones to boost weight gain.

GA1328

What about zoning? You bring up the Z word, but the bottom line is the same for any part of the law—the rules are fair only if the people who formulate them are fair and forward thinking. Where was the zoning board when this development was put up? Buying big cars with their kick-back checks? Where was MacDonald, by the way? You can bet that he wouldn't be happy to hear the housing was going in next to his alfalfa— no farmer in his right mind wants suburban kids on ATV's tearing up the winter wheat, and letting their untrained dogs run loose on his land to attack livestock.

(Study question: What is the long-term cost to society when high-quality farmland is developed for housing, and less fertile land is used for raising food—which requires use of more fertilizers, pesticides and herbicides?)

I know this is a diatribe rather than a critique, but these are issues which are currently being fought out piecemeal in the courts when, in fact, there is urgent need for broad-based policies to be formulated in order to preserve the public interest. This in itself causes me some serious concern. We either dictate to our population and their development, or they dictate to us. So where are our famous rights to Life, Liberty, and The Pursuit of Happiness? Are these rights only a function of ample resources like land?

You can see why I like this story. It can be argued from many different positions, and you can drag in everything but the kitchen sink. (From the audience: "Yeh, what about the kitchen sink? You got anything against plumbing?" Threats of union reprisal offstage . . .) So I will ask please, please, if you can bear the thought, go back, tighten it up, focus on MacDonald as a hardworking agri-operator and Marlene Jones as the single mother of four who is worried about her son's asthma getting worse since they moved near the farm. Let the kids play with the pig theme. Building dramas about the "Swinal Solution" and "Neither a lender nor a farrower be" are fun, but you have more important things to talk about.

Your sincere and loquacious critic,
Lorene Sterner

Reprinted with permission of Lorene Sterner, 1990, Ann Arbor, MI.

A Tail with a Twist

Point of View—Discussion Questions:

1. After the homes were bought in Fragrant Meadows and the families moved in, they complained that Farmer MacDonald was creating a serious nuisance. The worst part was the health hazard. He sprayed chemicals on his crops which were carried by the wind to the new houses. He often plowed his fields with a noisy tractor early in the morning and woke up the entire population. Besides all that, his animals stank. In the face of such strong evidence, how could the Civic Executive Committee decide in favor of Old Mac's right to stay?

Possible Answer:

The legal concept of "coming to the nuisance" is illustrated by this story and that is what made the difference in the decision. Old MacDonald was there first! The pig farm had been established far from the city for many years. Eventually the city spread out and finally came to the nuisance! It was the builders, after all, who made the independent business decision to develop the subdivision right next door to Oinker Acres.*

2. In what ways could the local environmentalists be unhappy with the threat to the environment created by all the people involved: the farmer, the developers, and the home owners?

---

*Greta B. Lipson, Ed.D., and Eric B. Lipson, J.D. *Everyday Law for Young Citizens* (Carthage, Illinois: Good Apple, Inc., 1988).

3. MacDonald, the pig farmer, was criticized by his farmer friends for refusing to go forward with change and "progress." It was their assumption that if the community experienced change and expansion, it automatically meant benefits for everyone. But does change always mean something better? In what ways can technological progress create serious social problems?

- Change can cause unemployment as people are replaced by machines.
- Change can also create more employment with greater demands on industrial energy which in turn creates more pollution and industrial wastes.
- These factors, above, affect the food we eat and the air we breathe.
- Technology in its march forward may bring the destruction of natural resources.
- The incursion of new construction can be a threat to the survival of wildlife and the delicate balance of the food chain.
- As a community grows, the costs of institutions and services increase. This creates a greater need for tax support, which in turn requires more business and industry.

GA1328

A Tail with a Twist

Improvisation—Role-Play Variations:

1. Role-play the Civic Executive meeting with all parties represented: farmer MacDonald and his wife Trichina; the residents of Fragrant Meadows; the land developers; and the residents of the city of Suidae, Iowa. Each group is there out of self-interest. Select a person to chair the meeting who can control the group, mediate trouble, and ensure a fair hearing for all.

2. Enact a different citizens' meeting. One group of good citizens are unemployed. They are in support of the Bud Pozey Land Developers coming into town, putting up a big shopping mall, and building homes, schools, and roads. They are opposed to a city building code which would limit and prohibit these sweeping plans for construction. They believe that the most important issue is employment which would be guaranteed by Pozey's ambitious plans. A different group of good citizens are in favor of a restrictive building code. They are very worried about the destructive effects of major construction on their community. They ask the question: How can we resolve the problem of unemployment and still protect the beauty and integrity of the town and its woods and lakes?

3. On Earth Day, April 22, you and a group of friends organize a committee to heighten the awareness of the community to the dangers of pollution. The name of the new organization is Protect the Interests of Good Environment, for which the acronym is P.I.G.E. (pronounced piggy). Your group is mainly concerned about the big imposing smokestacks of the local electric power company which belch smoke and spread pollutants and acid rain. Your committee has the inspired idea to have a big megawatt rock concert to protest the dangerous smoke and enlist the support of the people. The local electric power company sends a spokesperson to talk to you about your slamming his company. He points out to you that the energy needed to give electric power to the rock group for their musical extravaganza will be produced in his coal-fired plant. What does each side of this dilemma (the committee and the electric company representatives) have to say to each other?

GA1328

A Tail with a Twist

Writing Suggestions:

1. We live in a free society where the law functions to balance the rights of property owners who have different interests from each other. Concerning the limits to freedom, there is an expression in the law that says: "One person's rights extend only as far as the other person's nose." How would you explain that quote in a short paragraph?

2. After discussing "A Tail with a Twist," you have heard arguments for and against progress: the advantages of more jobs due to change, the effect of change on the environment, and the quality of life in the present and the future. If you had to identify your strongest bias relative to these issues, what would it be? Begin your paper with the header: "I feel most strongly about the importance of . . . (employment, environment, balance, etc.).

3. Just for the fun of it, read through the story "A Tail with a Twist" and make a list of all the words which suggest or remind you of pigs! Watch for some scientific or technical words as well. If you encounter fancy-sounding names or strange words, you may need the dictionary or an encyclopedia. Of course, people who live in Iowa may not have any trouble at all. Why is that true?

   Words from the Story That Suggest Pigs:
   tail; pigheaded; oinker; fragrant; shoats; sausage; Trichina; Barrow; sow's ear; piglet's snout; porcine; porker; barbecue; Francis Bacon; slops; sty; Hamilton Hocks; bore; hogwash; Suidae, Iowa (a fictitious place); hog-tied; lard . . . .

4. Add your own sentence or paragraph to any part of the story in which you include references to pigs. It must make sense in the context of the story. For example:

   - The families picnicked at Porker's Park on Loin Lagoon.
   - Professor Avoirdupois did research on hogs.
   - Everyone in town shopped at the Pig Wiggle Food Mart.
   - They liked to pig out on barbecued ribs.

GA1328

Chapter 12
A Tail with a Twist
Contentious People May Be Pigheaded
Student Comment

Characters: Mr. MacDonald, a pig farmer   Residents of Fragrant Meadows
             Trichina, his wife   Mr. Hamilton Hocks
             Farmers   Citizens of Suidae, Iowa

. . . .

   In a paragraph express your feelings about any aspect of this story which you liked or disliked. How would you have changed it?

Alternative: Now that the story has been discussed, explain the proverb above from your point of view.

. . . .

_____

_____

_____

_____

_____

_____

_____

_____

_____

_____

_____

_____

_____

_____

_____

_____

_____

GA1328

Award for the Outstanding "Tale with a Twist"

Award to: _____
(name)

For: _____
(title of story)

Room: _____

Teacher: _____

Signed and sealed on this date: _____

_____School

GA1328

Bibliography

Alter, Jonathon. "When Photographs Lie," *Newsweek*, July 30, 1990, p. 44.

Associated Press. News Features, 50 Rockefeller Plaza, Floor 6, New York, New York 10020, "Photo helps to clear man; he heads back to school," *The Detroit Free Press*, Saturday, May 26, 1990, page 13A.

Author unknown. "Sand Art, on Deadline," *The New York Times,* August 13, 1989, Section 22E.

Goldstein, Eleanor C., editor. *Social Issues Resources Series, Inc.* Boca Raton, Florida, P.O. Box 2507.

Gordon, Jeanne. "Teaching Kids to Negotiate," *Newsweek,* April 23, 1990, p. 65.

Hawthorne, Nathaniel. "David Swan," *The Complete Short Stories of Nathaniel Hawthorne: Seventy-Two Tales of Fantasy and Imagination.* Garden City, New York: Doubleday and Company, Inc., 1959.

Lasica, J.D. "A Picture's Worth 1000 Lies. New digital technology is challenging journalistic ethics," *Sacramento Bee*, October 9, 1988, Forum Section, p. 1.

Lipson, Greta B., and Eric B. Lipson. *Everyday Law for Young Citizens.* Carthage, Illinois: Good Apple, Inc., 1988.

Lipson, Greta B. *Famous Fables for Little Troupers.* Carthage, Illinois. Good Apple, Inc., 1984.

_____. *Fast Ideas for Busy Teachers.* Carthage, Illinois: Good Apple, Inc., 1989, p. 13.

Lipson, Greta B., and Sidney M. Bolkosky. *Mighty Myth: A Modern Interpretation of Greek Myths for the Classroom.* Carthage, Illinois: Good Apple, Inc., 1982.

Montague, Ashley, and Edward Darling. *The Ignorance of Certainty.* New York: Harper and Row, 1970.

Powers, Ron. "Do Teens Hunger for Heroes?" *Seventeen,* July 1981, p. 108.

Service, Robert W. "The Cremation of Sam McGee," *Collected Poems of Robert Service.* New York: Dodd, Mead & Co., 1940.

Vitz, Paul C. "The Use of Stories in Moral Development," *American Psychologist.* Vol. 45, No. 6., Washington, D.C.: American Psychological Association, Inc., June 1990, pp. 709-720.

Yolen, Jane, editor. *Favorite Folktales from Around the World.* New York: Random House, 1986.

Zablit, Jocelyne. "Where are the prizes? 3 charged with scam," *The Detroit Free Press*, June 1, 1990, Section 2B.

GA1328